Julia Foster's
PATCHWORK

Julia Foster's PATCHWORK

Her own ideas for you to make

Photographs by Christopher Cormack

Drawings by Caroline Holmes-Smith

ELM TREE BOOKS · LONDON

First published in Great Britain 1985
by Elm Tree Books/Hamish Hamilton Ltd
Garden House 57–59 Long Acre London WC2E 9JZ

Book design by Norman Reynolds

The Bride's Quilt, Bird of Paradise on p. 99 is
reproduced by courtesy of the Museum of
American Folk Art

British Library Cataloguing in Publication Data

Julia Foster's patchwork.
1. Patchwork – Patterns
I. Title
746.46'041   TT835

ISBN 0-241-11673-2

Typeset by Rowland Phototypesetting Ltd, Bury St Edmunds, Suffolk
Printed and bound in Spain by
Cayfosa Industria Gráfica, Barcelona
Dep. Leg. B · 26857·1985

Contents

Introduction 7

Simple Quilt 9
Tamara's Pink Satin Waistcoat 15
Woven Ribbon Quilt 19
Tricia's Garden Quilt 25
Lego Bag & Peg Bag 30
Liberty's Towel 36
Paper Patchwork Tray 39
Pink Hankie Cloth 43
Wicker Chair 46
Seminole Deck Chair 51
Painted Game Board 57
Baby's Puff Patchwork Quilt 61
Petal Picnic Cloth 66
Liberty & Old Lace 73
Sunburst Cloth & Quilt 79
Appliquéd Iris Quilt 87
Pink Baskets Quilt 93
Felt Appliqué Quilt 99
Harlequin Fancy Dress 105
Quilted Basket 113
Kite 117

Words of Advice 126
Glossary 127
Useful Addresses 127

Acknowledgements

My special thanks go to Christopher Cormack and Caroline Holmes-Smith who have made this book so gorgeous to look at.

My first patchwork

My on-going heirloom

Introduction

I know it sounds old-fashioned or maybe it's just 'post feminist' but my priorities are my husband, my children, my home and even my dog. For better or worse I have basic homemaking instincts that I enjoy fulfilling.

I was lucky indeed that my career as an actress was well established by the time I started having babies. I had already made films like *Alfie* and *Half a Sixpence*. It meant that I could continue acting at my own pace and in my own time. It also meant that I didn't have to consider giving up my career.

If you are going to try to combine motherhood with a career it seems to me that being an actress makes it easier than following any other career. During long runs in the theatre I have my days free. Television and film work is usually done in a few intensive weeks leaving 'parenting' time in between. I know I would have found it difficult to come to terms with a career that kept me away from my children all day, every day.

However good you are at combining bringing up children with maintaining your career, it makes for a hectic life. I have two young children at two different schools, a teenage daughter at a third, a boisterous young golden retriever, a vocal African grey parrot, a less vocal but equally attractive husband, a home in London to look after and a career sandwiched somewhere in the middle (Shakespeare soliloquies learned word perfect between cooking the fish fingers and doing the Latin homework). How on earth I find time to sew as much as I do I don't know, but sew I do! Anywhere. Anytime. And most important in any mood. There are only a few intermittent islands of tranquillity in my life.

I have sewn since I was a child. I was taught by nuns at the convent where I went to school in Brighton. I remember being made to undo hemming again and again to resew it with stitches so small you couldn't see them. I hated that sewing but years later realised what a gift they had given me. I could make anything! At least that's the way they made me feel. I could cut my own patterns, roll hems, embroider, do drawn threadwork, tat and make lace. Just show me something and I could make it.

Like any normal teenager I became obsessed with clothes. My sister Alex and I never went without, but there was little money for extras and my father eventually got exasperated at my constant whinging about clothes. 'If you want it why don't you make it,' he told me.

A whole new world opened up for me. I started making clothes not only for myself but for my mother and my sister. And when I was 16, after making quite a few things, I sewed all the leftovers together into a patchwork skirt. My first patchwork. My mother, who keeps nothing, carefully tucked it away in a bottom drawer after I left home and saved it. My eldest daughter found it years later and used it for 'dressing up' and I discovered that my fondness for patchwork went back much further than I had realised.

I am an obsessive collector. When I was a child I collected silver paper and shells and when I grew up and married, the silver paper became silver art nouveau brooches and the shells became shell pattern Belleek cups and saucers. I've collected old linen and lace, embroidered samplers and patch-work quilts.

After I married Bruce, we started visiting America quite often. In New York in 1972 Bruce bought me my first old American quilt, a 'Grandma's Flower Garden' pattern. Another obsession began! I fell in love with traditional American quilts.

It's a constant pleasure being able to sew things; to make presents for weddings and new babies. My children tell me I'm a great success with fancy dresses. I've produced witches' hats, cloaks, butterfly wings, a Twenties dress (made in the stalls of the Lyric Theatre Hammersmith during a technical rehearsal) and an Alice in Wonderland dress (made between fighting battles as Queen Margaret in *Henry VI*). My greatest achievement was to turn my son Ben into a crab.

Whatever I make, whatever I sew I always return to patchwork. If I'm making something for myself (which isn't that often) it is always patchwork, even if it's my own idea – such as the woven ribbon quilt I made for my dressing room (see page 19). Making patchwork still gives me the greatest pleasure.

At least twenty years ago I started a hexagon patterned quilt with fabrics that meant something special. When I look at it I can see a dress I wore in a play; a summer dress of my mother's; my sister's flowered shirt; little turquoise bells from a cushion I made to say thank you; Deborah Kerr's curtains and Emily's Biba dress – it just goes on and on. It still isn't finished – I add a few hexagons every now and then. The children call it my on-going heirloom. I really do sew anywhere, standing up during spare moments, while cooking, in the car while waiting for the children outside school or at the cricket pitch or the riding stables, on trains or on planes. Through mutual agreement with my husband there is only one place where I do not sew patchwork.

I probably do most of my sewing in rehearsal halls and theatre dressing rooms but wherever I sew I always enjoy it. I sew because I enjoy the actual sewing and I look forward to the finished product. Nothing I make is perfect but that isn't my objective. To some people I'm an actress, to three I'm a mother and to one I'm a wife. What I'm not is a professional sewer. You know you can always find time for sewing if you really want to. I mean, look at me. And the busier your life is, the more satisfying it is to turn round and say, 'Well actually, I made it.'

Simple Quilt

(that even my mother could make)

A good test for a simple-to-sew quilt is whether my mother could make it. I spent my childhood in Brighton with my sister Alex and our funny fox terrier Andy. My father was one of six children, and his mother, my grandmother, was called Peter and lived nearby. I've no idea how she got that name but I do know that she was always making things. One Christmas Peter made all of her granddaughters tartan kilts. She could sew anything and so, as it turned out, could my father.

As I said, I started making clothes for myself when I was in my teens. My father was fascinated with what I was doing and started helping with bits and pieces. He eventually became so good that he made himself a three piece suit and he made my daughter Emily a little camel coat. He was wonderful. There is no need to ask, 'Where did you get it from?'

I can't remember ever seeing my mother sew, however. She does lovely tapestry and makes the most mouthwatering, succulent classic English Sunday lunch but she does not sew. For my mother to make a patchwork it would have to be very easy, very simple and very quick.

Cutting up large squares and sewing them back together is the easiest patchwork process I can think of. You may have heard it before, but it reminds me of Maggie Tulliver's outcry to her mother about patchwork in *The Mill on the Floss*. 'It's foolish work – tearing things to pieces to sew 'em together again.'

If the quilt is to be as simple as possible it's important to use unusual fabric in really interesting colours. Without a doubt the most important part of making any patchwork is deciding on what fabrics to use. The more time and thought you put into this, the better. After all, if you are going to spend hours or weeks or even months making the patchwork and then years living with it, I think you should use the best materials that are available.

In searching for the unusual I found myself in Pimlico at a delightful shop called 'The Upstairs Shop'. Several years ago, I did a series called *Good Girl* for Yorkshire Television. I played Angie Botley, and it was the first time I'd acted opposite Peter Barkworth. The Upstairs Shop made me some lovely appliquéd cushions with the *Good Girl* opening credit cartoon motif and the words 'Good Girl' on them. I gave them as presents when the series ended. I always prefer to make my own presents, but there are times when I have to admit defeat.

The shop is run by Sheila Bloom. Her husband is a film editor which means that visiting the shop has the added bonus of a good gossip. I had thought that

I would use various shades of pink for this patchwork but when I saw their unusual apricot colour I changed my mind. I think they call it peach and it was mixed with an odd light green. There were so many co-ordinating fabrics that I found it difficult choosing only seven.

As I started cutting out the material I thought how nice a butterfly would look sitting in a square. A little piece of lace along a seam would be mouthwatering. As so often happens I was getting carried away with the extras. I can't help it. I love frills.

You can leave your simple patchwork plain if you like and it will still look lovely. My mother hasn't made a patchwork yet, but if she does she could make this one.

Instructions
You will need:
2 metres (78in) main fabric (for ruffle)
1 metre (39in) of each of 7 different but co-ordinating fabrics, 122cm (48in) wide
·5 metre (20in) iron-on Vilene
2·5 metres (100in) sheeting 230cm (90in) wide for backing
2·5 metres (100in) 4oz wadding
1 skein peach embroidery floss
Any odd bits of lace, ribbon or trimming

This quilt is made up of 63 squares of seven different fabrics 23cm (9in) square joined together with the sewing machine. Add a ruffle, which always looks good, and a backing, and it's finished. As you will see, I can never resist adding bits and pieces, but it would look just as nice plain.

Cut 63 squares 23cm (9in) by 23cm (9in), 9 out of each fabric.

If you want to, now is the time to add ribbons and lace edges to a few squares.

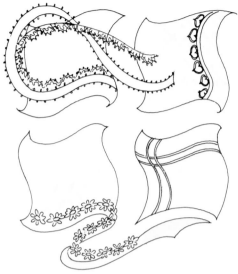

To appliqué some squares – I did four flowers and two butterflies – decide on a design and lay out enough of the co-ordinating materials in different patterns to be able to cut them out. Back this fabric with iron-on Vilene, using a hot iron with a damp cloth. Draw your design on the pieces of fabric and cut them out. Take the squares you are going to appliqué and back them with any rough paper, cut to size. Pin the paper in each corner. Glue your Vilene-backed pieces of design into place on the square with Pritt stick.

Machine round edges of stuck-on patterns using a very close-together zigzag and matching cotton thread.

Remove the paper from the back of the appliquéd squares – just tear it off next to the stitches, slowly and carefully.

Lay your squares out in a pattern that pleases you, using seven across and nine down.

Using 1cm (½in) seams throughout, machine stitch the seven squares in the top row together, and mark it 1. Then sew the next row of seven squares together and mark it 2. Repeat until you have all nine rows sewn together. Open all the seams and iron them flat.

Sew the nine rows together, open seams and iron flat. You have finished the top.

7·5cm (3in) wide is the perfect width for a ruffle. 5cm (2in) sticks out and 10cm (4in) flops. For a 7·5cm (3in) ruffle, you must cut strips 18cm (7in) wide and keep joining them until you have 1270cm (500in). Gosh, I thought, that seems a lot! I went back and checked, but it was right. If you measure round all four sides of your joined squares, it is 635cm (250in). For the ruffle to be really gathered, it needs to be twice that (that's why it takes two metres of material).

Join the ends of your strip. You now have a circle of fabric. A very large circle of fabric! Iron it all, opening seams as you go. Fold in half lengthways and pin. It's now 9cm (3½in) wide.

Divide the 1270cm (500in) into four and mark with crossed pins. Now divide the edge of your quilt into four and mark with pins. Using a running stitch and double thread, gather up a quarter of the ruffle to fit a quarter of the quilt, removing pins as you gather. Finish off with a couple of knots. Start again and gather up the next quarter of the ruffle to fit the next quarter of quilt, finishing off with a couple of knots. Repeat this twice more. The ruffle will now fit the edge of the quilt. The reason for this dividing is that very gathered material is difficult to control, and if the thread gets too long it will break. I have got into the habit of doing a section at a time, as it drives me mad if the thread breaks. Some people machine gather. I've never been able to get the fabric gathered enough – and I've had the thread break.

Take your patchwork top and lay it face down on the floor. Wrong side up, lie the wadding on top of it, making sure it overlaps a little all round. Wadding is never wide enough, so you have to join it. Butt the edges together and use large tacking stitches from side to side (see p. 103). Pin the wadding and patchwork top together round all four sides, and then sew. You can machine it. Cut off excess wadding.

Turn the quilt over – the right side now faces up. In half a dozen places, near the middle of the quilt, pin the wadding and top together, just to keep them in place while you put the ruffle and backing on.

Pin the ruffle on to the edge of the right side of the quilt.

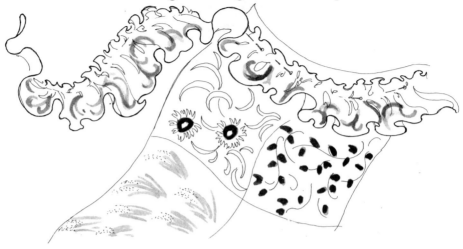

Machine stitch carefully round all four sides. Don't try to rush it.

Lie the quilt back on the floor, right side up, with the frill still turned inwards. Lie your backing fabric on top of the quilt and ruffle with right sides together and pin round three and a half sides (below left).

Machine stitch the three and a half sides and turn right side out through the half side that is not sewn. Turn in the edge of this remaining half side and sew it closed by hand. Lie the quilt out flat, facing you, and remove the pins you used to hold it together.

I then 'tuft quilted' it by tying the corner of each square with peach embroidery floss on the front of the quilt (below right).

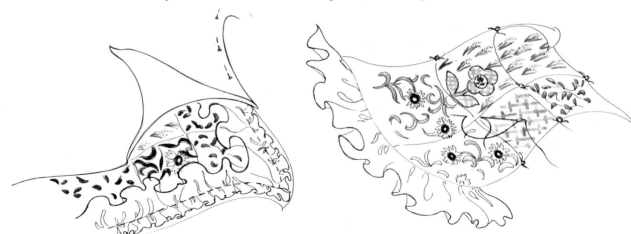

Tamara's Pink Satin Waistcoat

My daughter Tamara has an older brother and an even older sister. Being the youngest has advantages. There are lots of big people to look up to and be cared for by. But there are also hidden disadvantages.

When Tamara was three years old our family was invited, at short notice, to a Christmas party. I rushed out and bought her a dress to wear. Her little face lit up with amazement. 'Is this dress for me? Is it new? Did you really buy it just for me?' Well, my heart sank. Had I not bought her anything new before? I had not! She lived in hand-me-downs. Emily's things were gorgeous (you know how extravagant you can be with your first child), but they were still hand-me-downs. And in Tamara's eyes they were still Emily's. From that day to this I have been very careful about her having her own nice things.

Tamara used to be rather a tomboy and for practicality, lived in jeans and dungarees. But when she was about five, she discovered *pink*! Ever since then, if given the chance, she will never be out of it. If I want to make her something special it has to be pink.

Satin is, of course, a favourite with many young children. I'm sure the sheen of satin has a lot to do with it, but with Tamara, it's the texture that catches her fancy. She can lapse into a reverie by rubbing her cheek on satin.

I made this little waistcoat using an old tape lace waistcoat that I found many years ago. Now of course, not everyone is going to just happen to have an antique children's waistcoat sitting in their bottom drawer but it can be just as effective if you use a piece of new lace which you can get from the John Lewis curtain department.

The beading on the waistcoat comes from my bead drawer! I have leftover beads from necklace and bracelet projects, beads that I have bought just because they are so lovely, old beads for mending Victorian beaded bags and new beads from the Curve Lake Indian Reservation in Canada (near where my children spend the summer), used to decorate bark and basket weaving. Most of my beads have actually been given to me. It's really quite amazing what you are given when you have a 'certain' reputation. 'Don't throw that away. Give it to the squirrel. She'll find a use for it.'

Instructions
You will need:
1 metre (39in) heavy weight pink satin
1 metre (39in) curtain lace
All sorts of beads
A gorgeous daughter!

I didn't use a pattern for this little waistcoat. If you want to use one, then Butterick No. 6481 is good.

Cut out the back and two fronts. As I wasn't going to line the waistcoat, I double seamed the shoulders and side, so the raw edges were enclosed – satin does tend to fray. It just means you put wrong sides together and sew up on the outside, and then turn it the other way, right sides together and seam again.

From the lace, cut another back and two fronts about 2·5cm (1in) smaller all round than the pink satin. If you buy that heavy lace you can find in net curtain fabric departments, you can cut round some flowers, then you don't have edges to turn under (below left).

Join the shoulders and sides of the lace waistcoat.

Slip it on to the pink satin and pin. Hand stitch into place with tiny running stitches round armholes and all round front and back (below right).

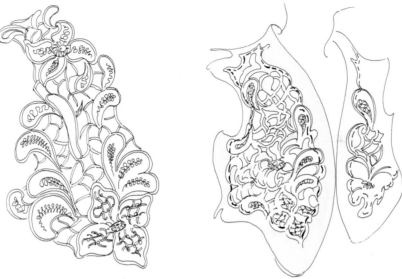

To bind the edges, I cut strips of the pink satin on the bias (cut across the grain of the fabric). I machine stitched it into place on the edge of the waistcoat, turned it over to the wrong side and stitched by hand.

Now for the part I'd been looking forward to, the beading. I love beads. I have a drawer full of nothing else, some in boxes, some in tiny polythene bags, some screwed up in tissue paper, some in throat pastille tins and some in Smartie tubes. Tamara thinks it's a treat to 'tidy the bead drawer'. We spent hours going through them. I would have used all pearls, but Tamara was mad about the shiny pink stars. Actually they look very nice.

There are several kinds of beading. If you are making necklaces and bracelets it's important to use the proper thread: most of it is nylon. Milward make terrific beading needles. (Actually they make terrific needles for everything.) They are very thin and have elongated eyes that accept the thicker thread. On Tamara's waistcoat I used white nylon beading thread and I made sure I knotted the thread between each bead. Knowing children, one bead is bound to get picked off or get caught on something, and it would be awful if they all came off!

Woven Ribbon Quilt

I very rarely make anything for myself. There is always someone else to make for: a birthday, a wedding or just school trousers to darn, track suit bottoms to tighten, hairbands to make. Sometimes there is simply no time to spare. I like my family's belongings to be spick and span and their clothes cleaned, ironed and put away. The drawback is that on occasion I've had to make a mad dash to Marks & Spencer for new underwear because mine is still at the bottom of the laundry basket.

When I set out to make myself a quilt I did so with a certain feeling of guilt. I was in the theatre at the time and decided my dressing room needed something – something special.

You'd be amazed how unglamorous most West End dressing rooms are. I've been known to paint mine from top to toe: after the reviews, I hasten to add! When you first arrive in the theatre you daren't do anything. You might have to move out in two weeks. You just wait. You do previews, you have your opening night and then you wait again, this time for the reviews, the daily ones and then the more important Sundays. Only then do you have some idea of how long you might be there. Only then do you really move in.

It's a good feeling being in a success. Your dressing room becomes a very personal home, a very special place; to use J. B. Priestley's expression, 'a magic place'.

Like my daughter Tamara, I have a passion for textures like velvet, satin and silk and we both love ribbons in our hair, on presents or turned into bows. I had often wondered what I could do with satin ribbons and on a previous visit

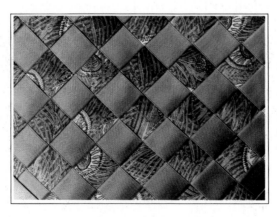

to New England I had been amazed by a unique and original quilt that had won a competition at a local county fair. The quilt was made with torn pieces of loosely woven linen with raw edges, woven together with pieces of velvet. An absolutely crazy combination. But it worked really well and gave me confidence to weave my satin ribbons with a mixture of cotton, silk and wool.

As a dressing room quilt it has proved an enormous success. It's something for people to talk about. Visiting dressing rooms at the theatre can be a difficult experience, even for me. I don't know why it should be so, but even if you have had a wonderful evening and enjoyed the performance of the actor you are visiting it still sounds cloying to say 'You were wonderful.' 'You were wonderful darling,' sounds even less sincere. My quilt is an ideal ice breaker. 'Oh, where did you get that quilt?' saves visitors from having to talk about the play immediately. 'Well, actually, I made it,' allows the conversation to take an easy line. It's a relief to have something else to talk about.

My first date with my husband started in my dressing room. I was appearing in the play *Lulu* by Frank Wedekind, at the Apollo Theatre on Shaftesbury Avenue. My dear dog Honey, who was then three years old, had been ill and I had taken her to the vet. As the days passed, and Honey got better I noticed how interesting the vet was! I knew it was not a time to sit about and wait to be asked out: he seemed quiet, intellectual, shy – and most unlikely to ask an actress to spend time with him. So I asked him if he would like to come to the theatre. Encouraged by the fact that he wanted only one ticket, I suggested maybe he would like to eat afterwards.

I was determined to make everything as ordinary and calm as possible. I told the stage doorman I didn't want any calls and all visitors were to be told I was busy. This was important business!

My plans were in vain. In the interval there was a message from my producer Oscar Lewenstein. His friend Joel Grey, who had just triumphed in *Cabaret*, was visiting from America, was in the audience and would be round after the show. Oscar had already put the champagne in my fridge and my dresser was busy laying out champagne glasses and rearranging flowers.

My heart sank even lower when during a quick change in Act Two I received another message. The writer Frank Marcus and his wife Jackie, my oldest and dearest friends, were at a first night next door. Frank was then drama critic on the *Sunday Telegraph* and they had heard that their friend Joel Grey was in the Apollo. They would join us afterwards . . . with a few friends.

The serious young vet was greeted by the most theatrical of scenes. The actress surrounded by writers, critics, producers and stars, all drinking champagne and being very flamboyant. Frank Marcus was introduced to Bruce. 'A vet, eh? Do you think you can tame this animal?' and he nodded in my direction. Everyone roared with laughter and poured more champagne. Somehow we survived that night, Bruce and I. It's funny how I knew how important it was even then.

Dressing room stories are wonderful and I should really be telling you how I made the quilt – but just one more. I had a fan, a middle-aged man, who visited the theatre every other night and sent me bowers of flowers. After some weeks I met him at the stage door and thanked him for all the flowers. 'But you really mustn't send me any more,' I said. His face fell and he looked sadder than a Basset hound. 'Well,' I muttered, backtracking, 'it's just that I don't have anything left to put them in.' The next day more fresh flowers arrived from Harrods together with a crate simply marked

VASES
ONE DOZEN
VARIOUS.

Instructions
You will need:
imagination
patience
a good cover on your ironing board

More seriously, you will need:
10 metres (11 yards) each of six different satin ribbons
1 metre (39in) each of six different matching fabrics
5 metres (5½ yards) 8oz wadding
5 metres (5½ yards) backing fabric (use one of the 'front' fabrics)
5 metres (5½ yards) iron-on fusable cotton
4 metres (4⅜ yards) satin material

I first chose six double-sided satin ribbons 2·5cm (1in) wide – three different greens – a purple – a burgundy and a plum colour. They were all as odd and unusual as I could find.

The difficult part was matching a fabric to each ribbon. I didn't mind what the fabric was, as long as it was patterned and matched exactly. (It was while I was trying to match these colours that I decided I was mad and wondered why I didn't just make an ordinary patchwork cover using a traditional pattern. Stubbornness got the better of me and I ended up with this strange selection of bits and pieces.)

Making the Squares
Make 24 squares, four out of each colour, as follows.
Take one colour of ribbon and cut it into 40 pieces each 24cm (9½in) long. Cut the matching fabric into 40 similar pieces each 24cm (9½in) long, making sure that each piece is 7·5cm (3in) wide.
Take each piece of fabric and, using a hot steam iron, turn the edges in

2·5cm (1in) on both sides. You will end up with 2·5cm (1in) wide strips that match the ribbons in size and weight.

Cut four pieces of fusable cotton, each one 24cm (9½in) square. On the ironing board (the one with the good cover) lay one piece of the cotton with the fusable side face up – looking at you. Take ten pieces of satin ribbon and lay them side by side on the fusable cotton, putting a pin at an angle at the top of each piece.

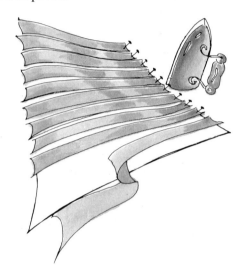

Take a piece of the matching fabric, weave it over and under the satin ribbons and pin each end.

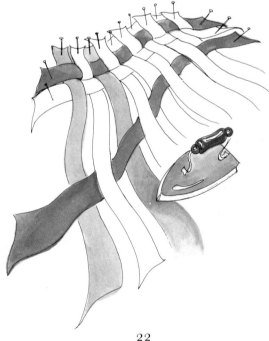

Continue with the remaining nine pieces, pinning at each end. Straighten the satin ribbons by pulling them gently downwards and pin them at the bottom.

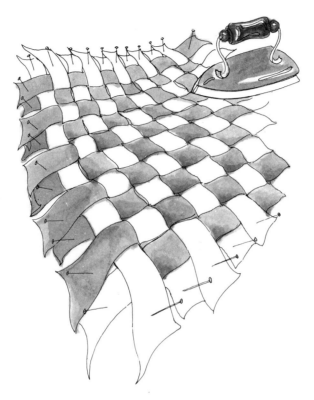

Having made sure that the ribbons and the fabric are in the right place, put a hot steam iron in the middle and iron out in each direction towards the pins. Remove the pins as you go and iron out beyond the edges.

The ribbons and fabric are now fused to the cotton and you can remove the completed 'woven square' from the ironing board. Make three more squares from the same colour combination.

Repeat this procedure and make four squares of each of the remaining five colours. You will end up with 24 squares.

This may sound repetitive, but in fact it's really fun weaving the ribbons and fabric together and the result can be stunning.

Putting the Squares Together

I chose a dirty green rather thin satin to join the squares. I cut 18 pieces of satin 12·5cm (5in) wide and 24cm (9½in) long. When I had done this, I realised that I had a problem joining such thin satin to the rather solid squares of woven ribbon so *I backed each piece of satin with fusable cotton*, too – boring but worthwhile.

Cut five strips of satin 12·5cm (5in) wide and 117cm (46in) long and join the strips of squares like this:

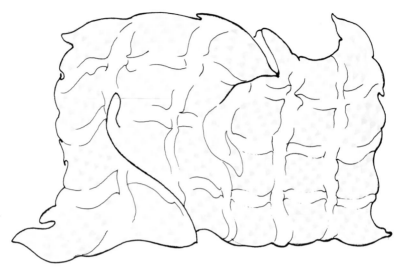

Add a 12·5cm (5in) wide band right round the edge. *Iron thoroughly. You don't get another chance!*

Backing and Finishing

Lay the quilt top, face down, on a hard surface. (I used the floor.) Put the wadding on top. It is necessary to join the strips of wadding. Do this by laying the edges close together and using a large tacking stitch, join one edge to another.

Pin the edge of the quilt to the wadding.

Cut the 5 metre (5½ yards) length of backing fabric into two 2·5 metre (2¾ yard) pieces, sew them together side to side and iron the seam flat open. I used that lovely yucky green Liberty print that I used in one of the squares. Lay the backing on the wadding, face up, seam down and pin all three thicknesses together (quilt, wadding and backing). Cut off the excess backing fabric and wadding.

The almost finished quilt looked so lovely I decided to finish the edge by hand.

Turn in 1cm (½in) of the quilt front and 1cm (½in) of the quilt back and, stitching through the wadding, join it all together.

I should have done the 'quilting' of the quilt by hand too, but I didn't. If you have the time to do so please do, otherwise machine around each woven square right along the existing seams. It works well and doesn't show. Stitching through the three thicknesses gives the effect of an old fashioned eiderdown. (See the instructions for my wicker basket, p. 113, for advice on quilting.)

Tricia's Garden Quilt

Over the years I have made all sorts of different quilts. Some were easy and some were not. Some took hours and some took months. If you hand sew a hexagon patterned quilt like 'Grandma's Flower Garden', it will take a lot of time and take a heavy toll on your fingers (I still find thimbles difficult to use). The first quilt that my husband Bruce ever bought me was a garden pattern and it's remained my favourite ever since.

Whenever I want something special in the way of fabrics I head for Liberty's or Designer's Guild. I've always felt that Tricia Guild designs especially for me because somehow she manages to design and co-ordinate exactly what I have been waiting for. (I'm also convinced that Ralph Lauren has been secretly living in my wardrobe for years.) Tricia Guild started the Designer's Guild in 1970 and has consistently produced exciting designs in wonderful colours. I don't know how she manages it but her materials are always very special.

Designer's Guild has fantastic sales, so if I can I wait for that twice yearly event in order to fill my fabric cupboard. Once a year nearly everything sells at half price – a really proper sale. It's probably not worth going on the first day, what with the queueing to get in and the football scrum when you do, because new sale stock arrives almost daily. If you can, buy remnants. That's the cheapest way. If you do you can acquire the best fabrics in the most wonderful designs at a fraction of their original cost – a good start.

I bought all the blue, purple and green fabrics to make 'Grandma's Flower Garden' this way and as usual I bought more than I actually need, to store some away in my fabric cupboard. The dandelion and thistledown are particularly terrific. I decided it should be Tricia's Garden.

It was difficult to decide what fabric to use with the 'glazed' Designer's Guild cottons. Plain white cotton looked dull, silk doesn't work with cotton and satin was quite wrong. I needed a sheen, not a shine. I was stuck, but then Professor Konrad Lorenz gave me the answer. Let me explain.

Two years ago, I accompanied my husband to a special birthday party in Vienna. The Society for Companion Animal Studies was holding a two day meeting there, to discuss the relationship between people and their pets, but also to celebrate the eightieth birthday of the Nobel Prize winner, Konrad Lorenz. We gathered at the Austrian Academy of Sciences, a marvellous 250-year-old building of marble and crystal and frescos, and listened to the Vienna Symphony String Quartet play especially for Konrad Lorenz. We

listened to laudations from the heads of the Academies of Science from eastern and western Europe and then we listened to this still handsome and articulate man describe how he originally became interested in animal behaviour. It was very moving. I knew I was being allowed to participate in a very special event and it filled me with joy.

I still felt this euphoria when I got up at 6:30 the next morning to go to the Vienna flea market. And I bought a little something. Damask! That's what was needed to complement the Designer's Guild fabrics! And I had two table napkins that I had bought on Konrad Lorenz's birthday in Vienna!

I experimented with a cushion by cutting the edges from the napkins and joining the two pieces. I appliquéd a flower hexagon that I had already made on to the napkin and used a matching blue piping made from cord and bias binding. The frill was added and it looked gorgeous. My problem, however, was that I didn't have any more damask. (I *had* in fact seen a *beautiful* damask tablecloth at that flea market in Vienna, but we had decided to indulge in an expensive meal instead. Next time my cupboard will take precedence over my stomach!)

John Lewis sometimes seems to have an answer for everything. Although they didn't have it in stock, they ordered it for me – white damask with a perfect sheen.

Instructions
You will need:
2 metres (2¼ yards) each of four different cotton fabrics (but I had some left over)
3 metres (3¼ yards) white damask for hexagons
1 metre (39in) blue glazed cotton
5 metres (5½ yards) white damask 150cm (60in) wide for backing
5 metres (5½ yards) 4oz wadding

When someone says 'patchwork', this quilt is what I think of. This is proper, traditional, hand sewn patchwork and absolutely gorgeous. I really love doing it, and I love the result.

You need two templates, one with sides 4·5cm (1¾in) long to cut papers and one with sides 6cm (2¼in) long to cut fabric. Many shops and mail order companies sell them – they are made of plastic or metal. You can make your own, but it is really worth buying some.

Don't try and cut too many hexagons at a time – they will not be accurate enough. The cutting out is most important and should not be rushed. The pleasure of the sewing later depends on it.

To make your hexagons, lay a paper hexagon on the wrong side of a fabric hexagon and pin it. Turn the fabric up over the paper and tack. Remove the pin (below left).

Sew hexagons together like this, with right sides facing (below, top right).

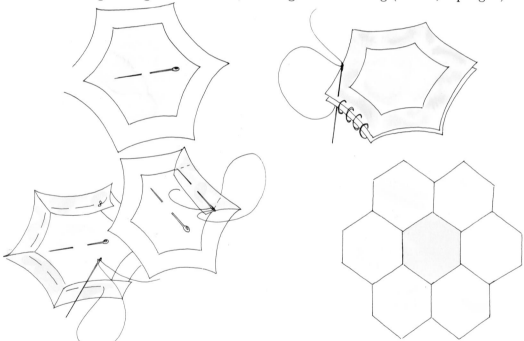

With Grandma's Garden, you make a number of 'flowers' and join them with white damask hexagons in between (above, bottom right).

You can make this quilt as big as you like by adding more hexagons. Remove all tacking stitches and take papers out.

I used white damask to back this quilt. It turned out to be rather expensive. I decided that when something has been hand made, maybe over many months, it deserves the best.

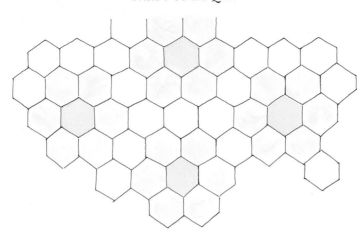

Join pieces of backing fabric together to make one piece the same size as your top. Open seam and iron flat. Lay right side down on the floor. Join the wadding, butt edges together and tack from one side to the other. Lay wadding on the backing and put your patchwork top, right side up, on the wadding. Pin round all four sides. If you have a quilting frame, now is the time to put it in. If not, use a large embroidery hoop and quilt from the middle out, using a tiny running stitch. Quilt round each hexagon (below left – I didn't do the white ones).

Bind the edges with a colour from your quilt. I used Tricia Guild's glazed blue cotton, which is in the middle of my flowers. Cut binding into strips 5cm (2in) wide and join them. Sew it on the edge of the quilt with right sides together. Turn it over to the back and hem under (below right).

Using hexagons is great fun and there is no limit to the patterns you can make. Or you can have no pattern – like my 'ongoing heirloom' quilt which is made exactly like Tricia's Garden.

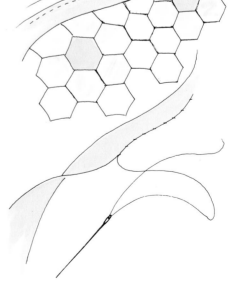

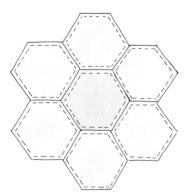

Lego Bag & Peg Bag

I enjoy playing with my children. An afternoon spent fishing or making a tree house or just colouring is time well spent. I enjoy their company. What did I do with my time before? It's hard to remember.

When Emily was born I had decided to continue working. I had known from the time I was thirteen that I wanted to be an actress and it seemed as if I had spent every second of every day since then working at becoming a good one. I got so much pleasure from acting that I sometimes felt quite guilty about being paid!

But now I had a baby. I decided quite simply to put my children at the top of my priority list and my career second. I didn't want to ever say to myself, 'Where were you when Ben took his first steps?' I didn't want to miss my children growing up and I knew I could reverse my priorities later when the children were older.

I suppose a part of us remains child-like even when we do grow up. Having children has been a wonderful excuse for re-exploring the pleasures of child-hood. Playing with toy cars – furnishing a doll's house – going to the zoo or the circus – waiting for Father Christmas or the toothfairy – building a snowman – going on boats and planes – all the things we take for granted as adults.

I was lucky enough to meet J. B. Priestley just before he died. I did his play *Time and the Conways* at Chichester and he attended a performance. When I knew I was to do this play I read all I could about Priestley and his strange theories about time. In doing so I realised that Priestley's plays were only a tiny part of this amazing man.

Priestley seems to have written about everything that interested him. I read his novels, his postscripts (a collection of broadcasts he made during the war) and his short stories. I think I gained most pleasure from a book called *Delight*, a large collection of essays about the things in his life that had given him delight. I responded to his every emotion, to each of his delights. If only I had met him when he was young!

In *Delight* there are several stories about the joy of children, the joy of playing games and the joy of remaining childlike. 'I would rather see one of my children's faces kindle at the sight of the quay at Calais than be offered the chance of exploring by myself the palaces of Peking,' he wrote. He also wrote, 'When I am playing with small children (and I am an old and cunning hand) I do all those things that bore or irritate me in my adult life. For example I plunge to their delight and mine into ritual and tradition, create secret societies, arrange elaborate ceremonies of initiation, invent mysterious codes and passwords. The most successful game I ever had with two of my children – and we played it every night for months just before their bedtime – was based on their remembering a monstrous rigmarole of questions and answers, which they often recollected when I forgot, that admitted them to some secret order we had cooked up between us. Their eyes immense, solemn, shining, they stood before me night after night motionless and quiet but poised on the edge of abandon – for if the ritual broke down anywhere they would throw themselves about and scream with laughter – and go through the maze of nonsense we had devised. This was how the day should end, and they were sharply disappointed if I happened to be engaged elsewhere; for they could not play this game by themselves and their mother, like any sensible woman, would have no truck with such solemn piffle, meant only for men and small children. Their delight brought me mine.'

Would he have been so lyrical about computer games, speak and spell or Lego? Maybe he would about Lego. It's wonderful stuff. I spend hours on my hands and knees building all sorts of dream buildings. I go on building long after the children have gone to bed and get into a terrible state when I discover that Ben has used all the flat pieces of red which my building depends upon.

Over the years I've made all sorts of drawstring bags to hold all sorts of things, scrabble, ballet shoes, swimming things, Tamara's collection of smelly rubbers, and Ben's collection of prehistoric sharks' teeth. This bag is one of a series of Lego bags. Blue top for the blue Lego, red top for red Lego and white top for white Lego (A mistake. It's filthy!). I wonder if my grandchildren will like playing Lego with a somewhat child-like grandma? I do hope so.

Instructions
You will need:
1 metre (39in) nursery fabric
0·5 metre (20in) matching plain fabric
30cm (12in) blue cotton
1·5 metres (59in) blue cord

Cut out a diamond-shaped template on a firm piece of cardboard, with each side measuring 13cm (5in).

Using the cardboard template, cut 18 diamond shapes from the metre of nursery fabric. I used a fabric with a rag doll design on it, so I cut out six diamonds with rag dolls and twelve from the rest (little houses and hearts). Cut 12 diamond shapes in the matching fabric. Lay them out like this:

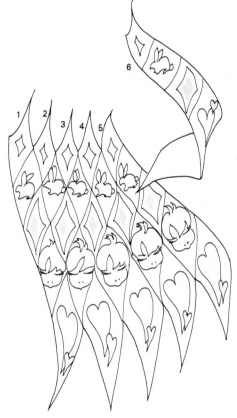

You will have six rows, each made up of five diamonds. Sew the diamonds in row 1 together, and repeat this procedure with each subsequent row. Join row 1 to row 2 and, ironing the seams flat as you go, continue until you have joined all six rows together. Fold the work in half, right sides together and join the edge of row 1 to the edge of row 6. This produces a 'cylinder' of patchwork. Cut off the excess diamond points on the top and the bottom.

Sew a seam along the bottom and it should now look like a bag.

Cut a piece of plain fabric 87cm (34in) long by 12·5cm (5in) wide. Fold this material in half lengthways and fold the two edges under 1·25cm (½in). Place the top edge of the bag on the material so that the top of the bag meets the edge of the 1·25cm (½in) fold. This means that the bag will overlap the material by 1·25cm (½in). Stitch all the way around, first at the bottom of the overlap and again, 1·25cm (½in) above at the top of the overlap. This leaves a 1·25cm (½in) tunnel to thread the blue cord through.

Peg Bag instructions
You will need:
·5 metre (20in) plain plastic
·5 metre (20in) patterned plastic
Polyester thread

Cut 13 squares of plain plastic and 13 squares of patterned plastic, all 10cm (4in) square. Using polyester thread, join them with the sewing

34

machine, making two separate pieces, like this:

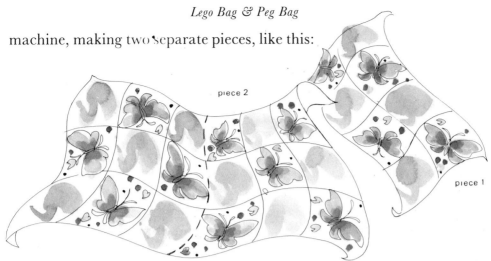

Cut a strip of plain plastic 38cm (15in) long and 2·5cm (1in) wide to bind the top edge of piece 1. Fold the strip in half, putting 1·25cm (½in) on the wrong side and 1·25cm (½in) on the right side. Machine stitch along, catching all three layers.

   Fold piece 2 in half. Lay piece 1 on top of it, and match the numbers. Pin it in place (below left).

There will be some spare plastic on piece 1 that will be sticking out – cut it off, then sew round the three sides (below right).

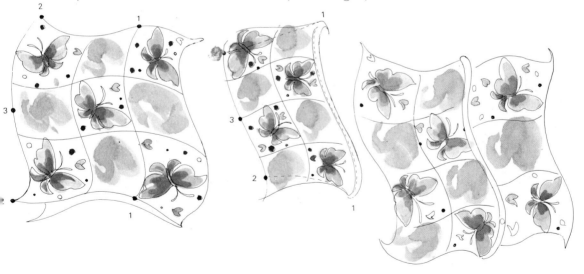

Cut three strips of plain plastic each 30cm (12in) long and 2·5cm (1in) wide. Bind the three sides in the same way as you did the top edge of piece 1.

   I used two green plastic pegs to hold it on the washing line.

Liberty's Towel

A few years ago Bruce and a marvellously dynamic woman, Babs Wright, set up a charity to train dogs for deaf people. Bruce and I had visited a training centre in Massachusetts some time before and had seen what good was being done there and Babs, who is Vice-Chairman of the Royal National Institute for the Deaf (RNID), already knew about the American training programmes and was anxious for help in getting one started in Britain.

Dogs are trained to respond to common household sounds. Quite apart from acting as 'ears' for the owner, a dog offers companionship. An owner and a dog can communicate with each other without words.

To celebrate their one hundredth anniversary, Marks & Spencer, who always give a lot to charity, decided to let their store managers choose local charities to give aid to. Hearing Dogs for the Deaf is a new charity and the training centre is near Oxford. The Oxford manager and staff decided that this was a local charity they would like to support and I was asked if I would come to Oxford, to their fashion show at the New Theatre, and receive a cheque for Hearing Dogs.

I'm a Marks & Spencer addict. I live in their Marble Arch branch, but I really didn't know what to expect from an M & S fashion show. I went to Oxford thinking as I got there that I should have worn something of theirs. I received the cheque, muttering that it was a relief not to be wearing armour (the last time I was in that theatre I played Shaw's *St Joan*) and Bruce thanked everyone concerned, on behalf of Hearing Dogs. By now we had learned that all the models in the show we were about to see, were actually sales assistants from various Marks & Spencer's shops.

We settled down to watch and I still wondered what we would see. It turned out to be an evening full of inventive surprises.

The girls were wonderful; all of them fit for professional modelling, but the surprises came with the babywear. Now I ask you. How do you model babywear at 9.00 p.m. when all good babies are in bed? They did it by having their range of babywear made in adult sizes 10 and 12 and worn by the girls. A gorgeous girl in a baby-gro with a pompom hat on is a sight not forgotten!

Marks & Spencer showed their range of sheets, pillowcases and duvet covers by turning them into crinolines, petticoats and dainty Victorian tops. They turned ready made curtains into men's suits, tea towels into miniskirts, and table cloths and napkins into bikinis and beachwear. It was terrific fun. Even food was modelled.

Turning something into something else has always appealed to me. Linen departments of big stores make my mouth water. The neat displays of piles of bouncy new towels and flannels in a rainbow of colours appeal to me enormously. It looks like someone's collection and I always feel the urge to buy some. What a good excuse to buy some flannels to turn into something else.

Instructions
You will need:
12 coloured flannels, about 23cm (9in) square
3 more flannels
cotton to match each flannel

Choose the colours you like best for what you will be using your towel for. White, navy blue and turquoise, for example, would be lovely for the beach.

Decide on the design of your flannels and lay them out. I used as many darkish colours as I could because Liberty has a passion for muddy puddles.

Overlap your flannels as little as possible, preferably less than ·5cm (¼in).

I took a yellow flannel and overlapped it with a tan one. This meant that the underthread of the machine had to be yellow and the top thread had to be tan.

Using a zigzag stitch, join two flannels together, and carry on until all the flannels are joined together. You will have to change the colour of the top and bottom thread with each side of each flannel but the result is very professional looking. In fact you shouldn't be able to see how they have been joined.

This is when I discovered I had a problem!

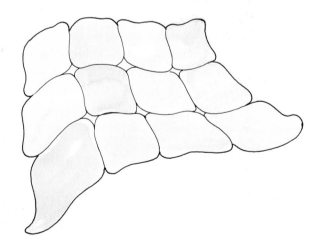

I had used flannels with rounded edges! There were holes in my towel – nasty empty bits. If I had used square flannels I would have been finished, but I simply hadn't concentrated when I was buying them, and had to devise a 'patch-up' job. That's why the instructions call for three more flannels.

Cut four 11.5cm (4½in) squares from each flannel. Pin them into place on the front and back of the towel, *covering the holes*, and stitch them into place using the same zigzag stitch.

Make sure you catch both the front and the back. I saved a piece of a cut-up flannel and made a thing to hang the towel up by.

Isn't it funny how things happen by mistake? It certainly wasn't planned, but the extra squares just finished off the towel nicely.

Paper Patchwork Tray

I had compiled about half the projects for this book when a friend of mine, a maker and sewer, came to see how I was getting on. She looked through everything very carefully and said, 'It's all marvellous . . . for people who can sew.'

Her words rang around my head. Everything I had made, I had made on the assumption that *everyone* can sew. I just took it for granted. 'Don't forget,' she said. 'Some people can't sew at all or can but won't.' Well, this patchwork is for the non-sewer. It uses paper, not fabric, and glue, not thread.

I have several trays tucked into a corner in the kitchen and I always seem to be using them for something or other but I've never really liked any of them. They are either too plain or too fancy. For this project I have used the plainest of my trays.

I was in Birmingham making *Late Starter* at Pebble Mill and I was pointed by Helen, who was looking after me (and my clothes) at the studio, in the direction of 'The Midland Educational Shop' to find the papers I needed. It was an enormous pleasure.

'The Midland' wins my prize for being the most useful, well stocked and interesting shop I've been to outside London and has charming, helpful and well informed staff. There are three floors, stationery, books and craft. The book floor is so well set out that even I could find anything that I wanted and it had a particularly good selection of children's books and a most comprehensive collection of art books. I had been looking everywhere in London for a series of Watson-Guptill's art technique books and found them at 'The Midland'.

To anyone like me the craft floor is Birmingham's heaven. It caters to graphic designers and to artists as well as supplying everything you can imagine for craft from coloured pipe cleaners to gold and silver imitation leather and fake fur fabric (for making rabbits and lions and other cuddly things). They supply glues, cutters, beads, even rivets for jeans. Every time I went in I discovered something else. I even bought a fishing bag that converts into a stool for my son Ben.

I had planned on using red school houses on my tray until I came across a matching set of wrapping papers in wonderful ice-cream colours. There was even a paper with clouds on it and others with flowers – perfect for the background to my patchwork picture. When I found those papers I suddenly realised how much I was looking forward to making a patchwork without sewing. It would be so quick; instant achievement. Done it!

As I sat peacefully gluing away, my mind wandered to all the other things you could make in paper patchwork. Boxes, fire screens, cork bulletin boards, even the inside paper lining of drawers. One day I hope to wallpaper a wall of my house (well, at least an alcove) in patchwork.

Instructions
You will need:
Sheets of wrapping paper (I used 7 sheets in different colours, but I had plenty left)
Pritt stick of glue
Household scissors (for cutting paper)
A plain tray
Firm paper to fit your tray
Glass, cut to fit your tray, with polished edges

Cut a piece of firm paper the size of your tray: mine was 30cm (12in) by 43cm (17in).

Some of the wrapping paper I bought had clouds on and some had flowers. I measured half way on my piece of paper and using Pritt glue stuck clouds at the top and flowers at the bottom. I then cut out two houses using five different wrapping papers.

Of course, you can make any design you like. Put all the pieces of paper together like a patchwork and glue them with Pritt glue on to the background (clouds and flowers). Place the finished picture in your tray and lay the glass on the top. There you are! Done. Quick and easy.

Once, quite a long time ago, Ben was ill and had to stay in bed. I brought him his meals on a tray just like this. I changed the picture with each meal, just simple things that were easy to do.

I remember he asked me to do 'Jaws' so it looked as if the shark was eating his supper!!

Pink Hankie Cloth

I mentioned that I'd appeared in the series *Good Girl*, written by Philip Mackie, with Peter Barkworth. When we finished the series Peter gave me a parting present, two glorious lustre bowls; one in pink and one in green. I just loved them!

Two years later I was browsing at an antique market and saw in front of me something that looked familiar. I stood there staring at this large pink bowl. 'Why is it so familiar?' I thought. Suddenly I realised that it was the same colour and pattern as the small lustre bowl that Peter had given to me in Leeds. 'There are more!' I thought, and that was the start of 'the Maling obsession'.

Maling lustreware was made in Newcastle-on-Tyne by a firm called . . . Maling. C. T. Maling started the business in 1859 and his three sons worked in the potteries right through to the 1930s. The lustreware that Peter had given me, and the bowl I saw two years later, were made during the 20s and 30s. Hundreds of different patterns were made in green, pink, pale blue and dark blue.

'The Maling obsession' soon spread. My husband contracted it first, then my children did. My mother succumbed and my sister followed her. Quite soon antique dealers throughout the south of England were appearing from out of the woodwork, with Maling in their hands and at ridiculously low prices. That was ten years ago. Today, as a result of Peter's gift, I have quite a collection.

Now what, you might ask, has Maling got to do with my hankie cloth? Well . . . recently I had the pleasure of working with Peter again, this time in a series

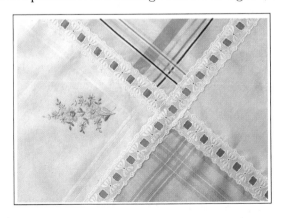

for the BBC called *Late Starter*, written by Brian Clark. When *Late Starter* finished I made Peter a blue hankie cloth for his seaside home. (I think the blue cloth is actually more attractive than the pink one.) I carried my tried and trusted Bernina by British Rail to Birmingham each time we went to Pebble Mill to record the series, and in the peaceful surroundings of the Holiday Inn I sewed away to my heart's content.

The blue hankie cloth was really lovely when I finished it and I thought I might borrow it back for a photograph, but I decided to make another one anyway. Pink was the obvious colour. There are hundreds of pink hankies about and it would look terrific with some of the pink Maling that Peter had been responsible for. So here is the cloth – and the Maling.

Instructions

You will need:

25 hankies 27cm (10½in) square – 12 pink, 12 white with pink flowers on, 1 dark pink
12 metres (13 yards) double edged broderie anglaise, that you can thread ribbon through
12 metres (13 yards) dark pink satin ribbon
6 metres (6½ yards) broderie anglaise edging

Decide on the design of your hankies. I laid mine out like this.

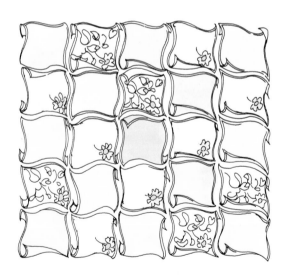

Cut four equal pieces of the double edged broderie anglaise, 28cm (11in) long. Take one of these pieces and lay it on top of the right hand edge of hankie number 1. Machine stitch together. Now lay hankie number 2 under the other edge and stitch. Repeat with hankies 3, 4 and 5.

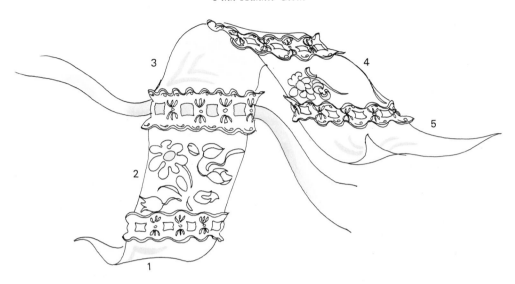

Repeat the same procedure with rows 2, 3, 4 and 5. You now have five rows of joined hankies.

Cut four strips of broderie anglaise 152cm (60in) long and join the rows together in the same way you joined the hankies.

Thread ribbon through the broderie anglaise and tack it at the outside edges.

Take the broderie anglaise edging, lay it on top of the outside edge and, using a loose zigzag stitch on your machine, stitch into place.

This cloth has proved really popular. All sorts of people have asked me to make them one. I am going to make one using antique lace hankies, all of which are a lovely creamish colour. There will be more work involved because first I will have to find hankies that are 'sympathetic' to each other and then alter them individually so that they are all the same size. When I make my antique hankie cloth I will dip the broderie anglaise in some weak tea to dye it. Cream coloured broderie anglaise is almost impossible to find.

Wicker Chair

A Contemporary Patchwork

The Quilters' Guild was formed in Britain in 1979, 'to promote a greater understanding, appreciation and knowledge of the art, techniques and heritage of patchwork; and to encourage and maintain the highest standards of workmanship and design in both traditional and contemporary work.' Both in North America and here traditional patchwork has been revived and developed further. There are all sorts of groups and classes teaching and talking patchwork all over the country. Here in London, 'The Patchwork Dog and Calico Cat', an enterprise run by Joen Zinni Lask, provides short but intensive classes in all forms of patchwork both for the beginner and the experienced sewer. Joen Lask has been directly involved in the revival of the Folk Art crafts here, was a founder member of the Quilters' Guild and has been its president for the last three years.

Contemporary works are full of self expression. Some comment on world problems, such as 'Nuclear Power' and 'Save the Whales'. Others comment on our lifestyle, such as 'Roller Skate' or 'MacDonalds Arches' or 'Tennis Anyone', a patchwork quilt covered with tennis racquets. Some celebrate modern technology. I like one of these that I have seen called 'Aeroplanes'. It's made up of twelve blue denim patchwork planes. In the future these contemporary quilts will undoubtably be regarded in the same way we regard the patchworks and appliqués of the nineteenth century, as evoking a bygone era, reflecting on life as it once was. Crafts people in the future will probably copy patterns like 'MacDonalds Arches', made from a repeating series of arch symbols, study them, talk about them, even form societies to perpetuate them.

There have been countless exhibitions of wall hangings, a popular form of contemporary textile art form, and patchwork clothes or 'wearable art'. Unlike our ancestors, there is no limit to what can be created but I always return to the traditional forms for inspiration and for ideas, although I admire those who don't. It would never enter my mind to make a quilt of a hamburger with a frill of green fabric in the middle representing the lettuce, but I enjoy seeing these patchworks.

I do however get these impulses to try different kinds of patchwork and it's surprising how many different techniques there are. Cathedral window patchwork is made out of folded squares that look like church windows when they are joined together. Crazy patchwork is created when bits and pieces are sewn, completely at random, on to a plain background. In puff patchwork like my baby quilt (p. 61), little bags of fabric are stuffed and joined together. Clamshell patchwork is a type of craft in which shell-shaped pieces are laid in overlapping rows. Suffolk patchwork is made with gathered circular patches sewn together on the edges and then mounted on the backing.

In Somerset patchwork squares of fabric are folded to make patterns. This is sometimes also called 'folded stars'. I decided to try this for a wicker chair that I was going to get at! I've always enjoyed origami and I imagined it would be a bit like that. It was.

Instructions

You will need:
A wicker chair, old or new
A cushion for the seat (cut to fit)
8 metres (8¾ yards) yellow satin ribbon
1 metre (39in) 8oz wadding
1 metre (39in) yellow taffeta
4·5 metres (4⅞ yards) Liberty print
3 metres (3¼ yards) cord for piping
1 40cm (16in) white zip
0·5 metre (20in) white cotton, 90cm (36in) wide

I covered a foam rubber cushion and made a backing for the chair before I made the Somerset patchwork, which I then appliquéd on to the back and seat.

It is quite easy to get someone to cut a cushion for a chair. Mine was 50cm (20in) by 46cm (18in) and 7·5cm (3in) deep. I made my own piping by covering cord with matching yellow ribbon. I cut three pieces of Liberty print, for the top of the cushion, the bottom and the piece round the sides. I machined them together with right sides facing and piping in between.

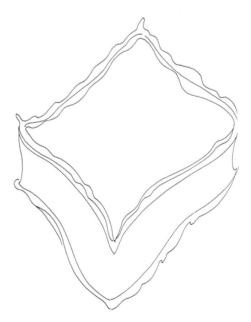

Sew round all four sides of the top, but only 3½ sides of the bottom. Pull right side out through the unsewn half side and sew together by hand.

On the back side of the cushion cut a 40cm (16in) strip to insert the zip.

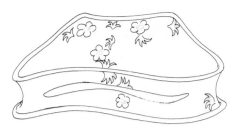

Measure the back of your chair, cut out two pieces of Liberty print to fit it and then cut a piece of wadding the same size and shape. Put the wadding between the two pieces, turn in the edges and machine stitch round. Sew yellow ribbons on.

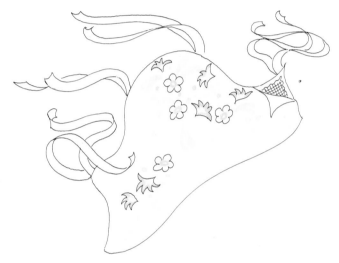

To make the Somerset patchwork, you need 40 pieces of Liberty print and 28 pieces of yellow taffeta each 13cm (5in) square.
    Fold each piece like this, ironing flat as you go:

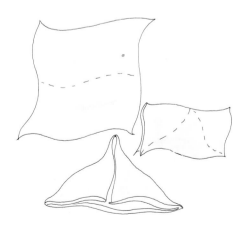

Cut the white cotton so you have a 46cm (18in) square. Using a pencil, mark it like this:

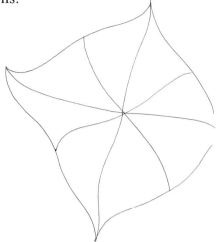

Lay four folded pieces in the middle of the cotton and sew round, by hand or with the machine. Add eight more with tips about 2·5cm (1in) from the middle and sew round.

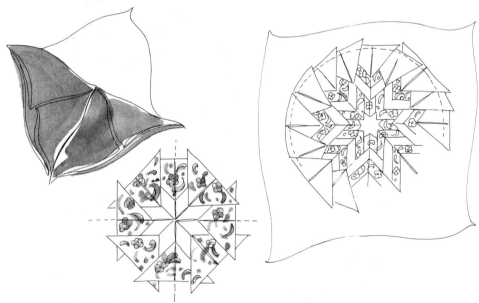

Continue until you have six rows. Cut off the excess white cotton, turn the edges of the last row of folded pieces under and sew into place on the back of the chair. Make another circle of Somerset patchwork for the seat of the cushion.

Using the yellow ribbons, tie the back to the wicker chair and put the cushion on the seat.

Seminole Deck Chair

Strip patchwork is a unique American folk art created by the Seminole Indians in Florida. What makes strip patchwork even more interesting is that it was invented deep in the Everglades of southern Florida by Seminole Indians, using sewing machines!

When the first explorers arrived in the new world of America there were no Seminole Indians but when white settlers arrived in what is now Alabama and Georgia, members of the Creek Confederacy of Tribes were forced to move south to the safety of Florida, which was still owned by Spain. These Creek Indians lived peacefully under Spanish rule and came to be known as the Seminole, which means 'wild people' in the Creek language.

In 1819, however, Florida became an American state and with time, the American government demanded that the Seminole Indians move with other tribes to the Indian Territory in Oklahoma. One group of Seminole refused and, led by a young warrior named Osceola, they fought an evasive war for seven years. In 1842, when by mutual agreement the war ended, several hundred Seminole remained deep in the Everglades, having never signed a peace treaty with Washington. Ten years later another war ensued and many of these survivors gave in and were moved to Oklahoma, but around 150 proud Seminole Indians disappeared further into the Everglades to remain there undefeated. In 1891 the government finally set aside land for them and in 1924 declared them to be citizens of the United States. It was during this period that the Seminole purchased sewing machines and developed strip patchwork.

The Seminole's forebears have a long history of using textiles. One of the first Spanish explorers in the area, Hernando de Sota, described Creek fabrics in the 1500s – 'large quantities of clothing, shawls of thread' made from the inner bark of trees and flax-like threaded out grass.

I never expected to discover that the Seminole originally made their intricate strip patchwork designs, deep in the Everglades, using Singer sewing machines but that is what can be so exciting or amusing about patchwork. They also had a passion for rickrack braid.

One year, after spending Christmas with Bruce's family on the Gulf of Mexico side of Florida, we had to drive back to Miami to catch the flight home and, as a special treat for my son Ben, we decided to drive through the Everglades along 'Alligator Alley'. One day this will no doubt be a boring superhighway but even now it is still a two lane road with nothing beside it except the occasional Seminole shanty where you may stop, look for alligators and buy Indian handcraft. We did stop and Ben did see alligators in the swamp and when we left I bought Tamara a sun hat. And it was ages later I realised it was Seminole strip patchwork! It even has rickrack, eleven bands of tiny rickrack braid and a little rickrack tassel at the top.

I've always wondered why deck chairs are so dull. Seminole strips would make a perfect seat for one, I thought. I set to work and when I had finished I had to restrain myself from covering it with rickrack.

Instructions
You will need:
An old deck chair frame
137cm (54in) deck chair canvas (I bought mine from John Lewis)
0·5 metres (20in) each of four plain cotton fabrics (I used dark and light blue, emerald green and yellow)
Blue gloss paint
Staple gun

I decided to make several strips of Seminole patchwork, join them together with plain bands of coloured cotton fabric and then stitch the whole thing on to the canvas.

The patchwork itself is made from fabric strips of varying widths which are machined together and then cut into sections and resewn to make strips of patterns.

The rows of joined strips can be cut and rearranged to produce an endless variety of patterns.

These are the four patterns I used.

Most plain cotton is 36in (just under a metre) wide. Cut your strips of fabric right across and they will all be 36in long.

For Band 1:
You need five strips of fabric:
     3 dark blue, 4cm (1½in) wide
     1 yellow, 4cm (1½in) wide
     1 green, 7·5cm (3in) wide
Sew together two blue and one yellow, then sew together one green and one blue. Use ·5cm (¼in) seams throughout.

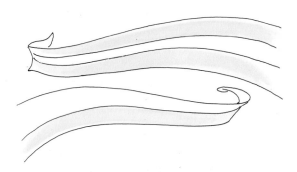

Cut each strip into pieces 4cm (1½in) wide

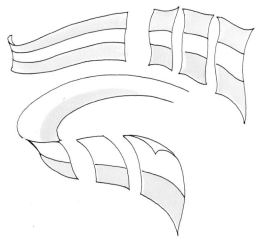

Turn piece 1 on its side and sew piece 2 on the top and bottom.

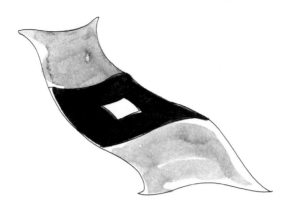

Make several pieces. Offset them and sew together like this:

Turn sideways and cut off the top and bottom.

For Band 2:

You need four strips of fabric:

    2 green, 10cm (4in) wide

    1 pale blue, 4cm (1½in) wide

    1 dark blue, 4cm (1½in) wide

Sew together like this:

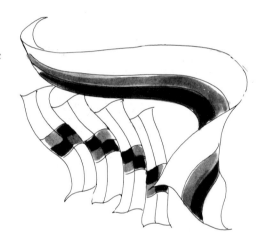

Cut the strip into pieces 4cm (1½in) wide. Turn alternate pieces round and sew together in twos – you will be putting a dark blue patch next to a light blue one.

    Make several pieces and sew together, offsetting like this:

Turn sideways and cut off the top and bottom.

For Band 3:

You need 5 strips of fabric:

    2 dark blue 4cm (1½in) wide

    1 yellow 4cm (1½in) wide

    2 pale blue 4cm (1½in) wide

Sew together like this:

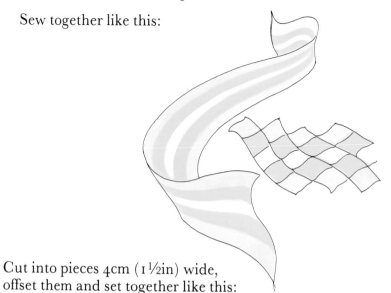

Cut into pieces 4cm (1½in) wide,
offset them and set together like this:

Turn sideways and cut off top and bottom.

For Band 4:
You need two strips of fabric:
    1 green 8cm (3in) wide
    1 dark blue 8cm (3in) wide

Sew them together and cut the strip into pieces
4cm (1½in) wide. Reverse every other one,
offset and sew together like this:

Turn sideways and cut off top and bottom.
    In my deck chair band 5 is a repeat of band 1 and band 6 is a repeat of
band 3.
    Join your six strips together with different width pieces of the four
cotton fabrics, whichever you have left.
    Lay the piece of patchwork on the deck chair canvas, turn the edges
under and hand stitch the patchwork fabric to the canvas.
    Paint the deck chair. Because the chair I used was new, Bruce primed it
first and then painted it with two coats of a gloss that I had mixed to
match the fabric.
    Using a heavy duty staple gun, staple the patchwork canvas on to the
deck chair frame.
    Once I had finished this chair I wished I had done two or even three.
The other deck chairs look awfully dull.

Painted Game Board

As a Christmas present to each other, Bruce and I spent a weekend in New York one December. Amidst the Christmas crowds and Christmas decorations and Father Christmases at every street corner we made our way to the American Museum of Folk Art to see an exhibition of old game boards. I really didn't know what to expect.

The decorative folk art quality of the game boards came as a revelation. 'Just like patchwork,' I thought. Some boards were painted, others were inlaid or carved or were made of applied material or were combinations of these techniques. The decorations themselves had nothing to do with the playing of the game: they seemed to exist for their own sake, for the pleasure of the maker and the players. Most were made in the nineteenth century and the most interesting came from Nova Scotia.

There are basically three types of games: opposition games, racing games and alignment games. Opposition games such as chess and checkers are those in which players attempt to capture or immobilise their opponents through a system of strategic actions. Chance is not a factor.

Alignment games like poker, scrabble and The Mill Game involve the players in attempting to place objects in a specified configuration. Both chance and strategic actions can influence the outcome in these games.

In racing games such as backgammon and Parcheesi, players race along a given track, the first player to complete the course being the winner. Action is controlled by devices like dice and spinners which offer each player an equal chance.

Racing games have been played throughout the world for centuries. There are surviving examples from many ancient cultures. Some from as early as 3000 B.C. have been found in burial mounds and Egyptian tombs. Most of the commercially printed game boards that are sold today are nothing more than modifications of ancient racing games.

The basic form of a Parcheesi racing board is a cross with each of the four arms made up of three individual columns. In each column there are eight moves making up 24 moves in each arm.

In the last years of the nineteenth century a British manufacturer patented one of these games and called it Ludo. With a few differences Parcheesi is simply an old-fashioned form of Ludo. Ludo has 18 moves in each arm and is played with only one dice.

The game boards that we saw at the Folk Art Museum were marvellous because they were functional and at the same time aesthetically so pleasing. I literally floated out into the frosty air with only one thought in mind – how soon could I make one! A little house representing home in the middle of a Parcheesi board from Nova Scotia is what gave me my inspiration to make this one.

Instructions
You will need:
A piece of laminated pine 2cm (¾in) thick, measuring 53cm (21in) by 53cm (21in)
Primer
4 small cans vinyl silk emulsion: red, green, brown and beige
A bevelled ruler (see-through plastic is best)
Compass, pencil and soft rubber
1cm (½in) paint brush
2 thin paint brushes (children's water colour brushes are perfect)
An old saucer
A Stabilo broad black water-resistant pen
Picture framing

You can't buy a piece of pine wood 53cm (21in) wide. I didn't know that. When you think about it, it becomes obvious – there aren't many pine trees with trunks that big. The answer is joined strips, laminated pine. The wood yard I went to sold it 2cm (¾in) thick and 53cm (21in) wide, but 178cm (70in) long. I asked them to cut it into three – I can always make a chess board, or snakes and ladders, I thought. Actually, the two spare boards still fall out of my odd cupboard every time I open the door.

When I got home and measured my board, it was 53cm (21in) by 58·5cm (23in). Hell – not square – serves me right for saying 'Cut it into three' without thinking. I wasn't going back to have a couple of inches cut off, I would manage. If you look at my games board you will see an inch-wide band of brown down two sides!

If you can, get a square piece of laminated wood 53cm (21in) by 53cm (21in). On a large piece of newspaper, paint one side of the wood with wood primer and leave it to dry.

Using a ruler, compass and pencil, mark the board out like this on the primed side.

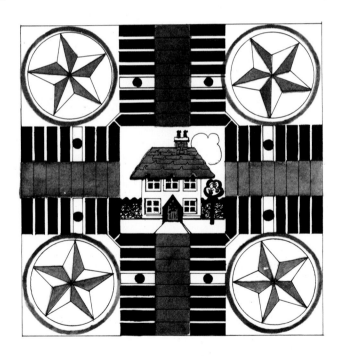

Paint one colour at a time. I used some of my thinnest oil-painting brushes, but any children's paint brushes will do. For the larger areas you can use a 1cm (½in) brush. I found a can of vinyl silk, even a smallish one, unmanageable, so I got out an old saucer and poured a small amount on to it. Just right: I used it like a palette.

59

Paint all green areas first, then red, then beige and finally brown. Leave to dry between each colour.

With the green I needed to do a second coat. All the other colours were fine after one. I liked the slightly streaky look – it didn't look new or perfect. Oh yes. The windows of my 'home' are a mixture of beige and a tiny bit of brown. To do the black outline, I found Stabilos wonderful pens. Permanent, fade-resistant, water-resistant, you can use them on anything, it seems, even glass, plastic and metal. I used a broad black one. Using a ruler, outline the large squares and the eighteen moves in each arm of the cross. The pencil marks you put on the primed wood will still show through the paint: use these as your guide. It is very important to use a bevelled ruler, so that the edge of the ruler does not touch the paper as you draw along it (with this type of pen it would smudge).

I took my finished board to one of those places where you make your own picture frames. I chose a very plain wood frame and made it in the shop. They cut the frame for you and you hammer in the little things to keep the corners together. I slipped the frame on to the board and it fitted snugly. I came home smiling – I'd never made anything like it before.

Baby's Puff Patchwork Quilt

I have an amazing father-in-law. Forty years ago he built, with a hammer and a saw, a four-bedroom cottage by a lake north-east of Toronto. I've no doubt he could build another tomorrow if he were asked to. He has moved the boat house that he subsequently built several times for want of something to do.

Bruce and his brother and sister spent their childhood summers growing up in this very personal cottage and it was no surprise that he wanted our children to spend their summers there too.

Summers have changed very little in the cottage country in Ontario during the last forty years. There's the odd beep from a Pac Man, the boats have bigger engines, the cars in the drive no longer have running boards and . . . there is a television aerial.

When the cottage was built, my mother-in-law Aileen refused to bring 'civilisation' out to the lake. The cottage was for getting away from the city, for communing with nature. But Aileen is the youngest in her family and by the 1970s she had several brothers and sisters in their 70s and 80s. She worried that if something happened to one of them she could not be reached. And so reluctantly, but for peace of mind, she had a telephone installed. The dam was broken and the flood ensued.

Aileen's brothers and sisters are an interesting lot. In fact it would be more accurate to describe some of them as odd, eccentric and bizarre and none more so than Uncle Reub. Uncle Reub is in his 80s, bald, myopic, short with the stature of Buddha and without doubt one of the most attractive men I've ever met. He trained as a doctor in the early 1920s, perfected a technique for a bloodless tonsillectomy in the late 1920s, fell hopelessly in love with almost every beautiful woman he met (and married several), gave up medicine to travel the world with an opera singer and when he returned to medicine finished his professional career practising psychiatry.

Uncle Reub was coming to the cottage for several weeks but, not wanting to miss the Watergate hearings which were broadcast live each day, asked if he could bring a television along. The cottage is in the middle of nowhere and Aileen triumphantly agreed that yes he could bring a television but that he would be unable to receive a picture on it. With permission granted, Uncle Reub set to work and before anyone could blink had what can only be described as a television mast erected beside the cottage.

Many children have been grateful to Uncle Reub since then and even I have

enjoyed quite a few good films while staying inside nursing a sunburn, but this is not what Aileen thought a cottage was to be used for. Life at the cottage was to talk, to make and to do, not to go square eyed in front of a TV and Aileen, who is not one to do things by halves, decided to make a puff patchwork quilt for her daughter. She had seen a picture in a magazine.

All hell broke loose. Material was got from here and there. Anything that came to hand was instantly cut up into four inch squares. The treadle sewing machine whizzed away and little puffs flew in every direction. The children were issued with bags of wadding to fill the puffs and the pile of puffs grew steadily. The dogs pushed them around on the floor, the children went to bed thumb in mouth, puff in hand. I've never seen so many! Aileen drove in to Toronto, measured her daughter's bed and decided that the quilt had to reach the floor on each side; another 500 puffs.

So the summer progressed, no television, no frog hunting, just puffs. Aileen is the only person I know who is as obsessive as I am, and as fast! My daughter Tamara runs her a close second. The quilt was absolutely gorgeous and still is. I wish you could see it. Very large it is! My little baby's puff patchwork quilt is a memory of that summer.

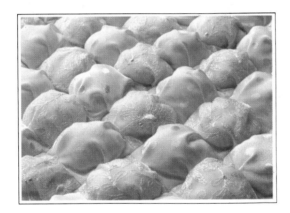

Instructions

You will need:
1 metre (39in) white cotton
1·5 metres (1⅝ yards) cream silk (that new washable kind), 120cm (48in) wide
0·5 metre (20in) embroidered muslin, 122cm (48in) wide
1 500gm (1lb) bag of washable synthetic wadding (you probably won't use all of it)

Puff patchwork is basically square or rectangular bags of fabric stuffed with wadding and sewn together. The back lies flat and the front is three dimensional and raised.

Iron all material carefully before you begin. You don't get another chance.

Cut the white cotton into 120 pieces each 7·5cm (3in) square. Cut one metre (or yard) of cream silk into 60 pieces each 10cm (4in) square. Cut the muslin into 60 pieces each 10cm (4in) square.

Take one square of white cotton and one square of cream silk and placing them back to back, pin them at each corner. Pleat the excess fabric at the centre of each side and pin each pleat. Using your sewing machine, stitch around three sides using a narrow 6mm (¼in) seam.

Insert the wadding through the open side, being careful not to stuff too tightly.

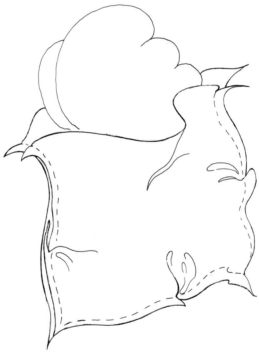

Make a pleat at the centre of the fourth side and stitch the side closed.

You have made a puff! Now make the remaining 119, 59 using silk and 60 using muslin.

You can make your quilt as large or small as you like by adding or taking away puffs. I used a see-through muslin because I had initially intended to stuff each puff with coloured wadding and wanted the colour to show through. You could have a haze of pink or blue for example. It didn't work with the cream silk so I used white wadding in the end. I'm still sure there's a lovely quilt to be made using coloured wadding.

I made this quilt 10 puffs wide and 12 puffs long.

Sew the puffs together alternating a silk one and a muslin one. Place them face to face and stitch them together over the previous seam. (It's easier than it sounds.) Sew 12 puffs together in a row. Make 10 rows of 12 puffs and then sew the 10 rows together.

Lay the quilt top on the remaining cream silk backing fabric, making sure that the backing fabric extends 10cm (4in) beyond the quilt on three sides and 20cm (8in) at the top, to leave a wider band there.

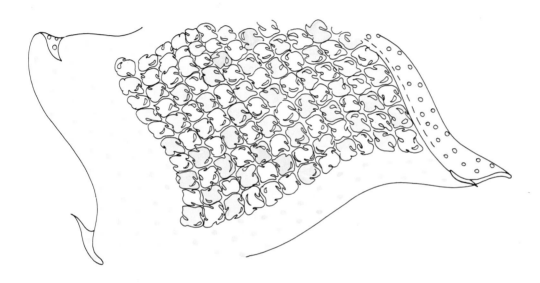

Fold the backing fabric up over the edge of the quilt, turn the edges in and stitch them. Done!

Petal Picnic Cloth

One summer we all went to Massachusetts. For several weeks we lived in a house in the middle of a forest near the top of Mount Everett in the southwest corner of the state, where Massachusetts, Connecticut and New York State all meet.

It was wonderful there. Emily went to summer camp and became 'very American'. Tamara and Ben went to day camp at a place with the delightful name of Buttercup Basin. Bruce was busy writing his first book, *Pets and their People*. He grew up only a few hundred miles away in Ontario and knew that there was a marvellous old library in nearby Lenox, a building originally built in 1815 as a court house and converted in 1873 to an elegant and homey library; a Federal style building with a most tranquil reading room.

All of my family had their own things to do and this meant that I was to be *alone*, for several hours a day and for several weeks. I was away from home, away from all the things I would have felt obliged to do had I been in London. It was wonderful!

I set myself all sorts of projects, but they were abandoned as soon as I paid my first visit to Stockbridge. I was happy to go no further! The place seemed perfect: a wide main street, a five booth diner with a soda fountain, the Mission House, the Episcopal Church with a

window by Tiffany, the Berkshire Playhouse and most important of all, the Red Lion Inn. The inn was famous long before Norman Rockwell painted it and is a large rambling white clapboard building with a huge porch facing Main Street. You can sit for hours in very old rocking chairs, just watching the world go by.

The present inn was built after a fire in 1897 but it had been an inn long before that, since 1773 I think. It has been added to over the years. The inside is filled with early American furniture and paintings and there is a wonderful collection of antique china. The first time I was in there admiring the eyes of a large brown cow in a folk art painting, André Previn brushed past my arm and disappeared through the screen door out into the sunlight. Different from early morning make up calls, school rotas and baked beans on toast!

All of this brings me to the other main attraction of Stockbridge, the reason why André Previn was staying at the Red Lion. Just up the road in Lenox is Tanglewood, the summer home of the Boston Symphony Orchestra. Tanglewood consists of 210 acres of glorious countryside with lawns, lakes, gardens, woodland and of course the theatre. It is here that the BSO hold their open air Summer Berkshire Music Festival. During the 1982 season, apart from the guest appearance of André Previn, they were celebrating the hundredth anniversary of Stravinsky's birth, with programmes and discussions of his work.

I remember the first morning I set out for Tanglewood as though it were yesterday. I can feel the heat and humidity. Programmes and seminars started at 10 a.m., all out of doors. 'Take a picnic,' I was told. 'Everybody does.'

I dropped Tamara and Ben at Buttercup Basin, dropped Bruce at the Lenox library, sent a letter to Emily and arrived at Tanglewood in the midday sun. Seiji Ozawa and the Boston Symphony were already playing. The sight was stunning. One side of the theatre was completely open and music spilled out into the sunshine and poured over the grass. And the grass! To the distant edges of the woods the grass was covered with patchwork quilts! I couldn't believe my eyes. There were old ones, new ones, appliquéd ones, contemporary ones, traditional ones, Amish ones and just plain quilted ones. Every kind you can imagine. They were covered with food and wine, babies and toddlers, dogs and birds in cages, young people, very old people, some American, some not, some in the sun, some in the shade of the huge maple trees. All listening to the music.

As you can imagine, the next few weeks were wonderful. I saw a lot of quilts, gained respect for Stravinsky, fell in love with Seiji Ozawa's back – such energy – and promised myself that when I got home I'd make a quilt or cloth that I would enjoy having a picnic on. I even plucked up courage to say 'Hello' the next time I saw André Previn at the Red Lion.

I did make my cloth, as you can see. I thought of taking it to Glyndebourne, but it wouldn't be the same without that marvellous harvest of quilts.

Instructions

You will need:

6 metres (6½ yards) of fabric (one metre (39in) of each of 6 different patterns), 90cm (36in) wide

2 metres (2¼ yards) extra of your favourite fabric from above (for use in the centre of the patchwork and for napkins)

6.5 metres (7⅛ yards) of lightweight (iron-on) interfacing

2 metres (2¼ yards) white sheeting, 90cm (36in) wide

6 metres (6¼ yards) bias binding

The Undercloth

To cut a round cloth, fold the white sheeting perfectly in quarters and lay it flat on a hard floor.

Tie a pencil to a piece of string and anchor the other end of the string, with a pin, to the corner which is the actual middle of the sheet. This should be done so that the distance from the pin to the pencil is 90cm (36in). Keeping the string taut, draw a quarter circle around the 90 degrees to the far corner. Carefully cut through all four thicknesses of the fabric (below left).

Open out and cut V notches into the raw edge about 1cm (½in) apart. Turn under a hem of ·5cm (¼in) and iron flat. The notches will close up to allow the fabric to lie flat (below right).

Stitch white bias binding on the wrong side of the cloth to cover the raw edge.

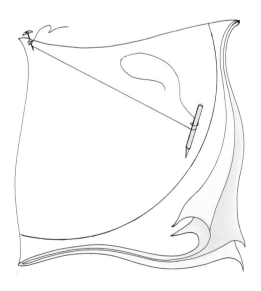

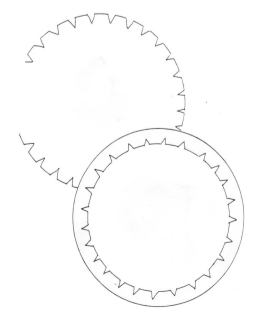

The Petals
I used these six fabrics.

Cut each metre of fabric into four 25cm strips.

Cut 24 pieces of interfacing the same size and iron a piece on to the back side of each of the 24 pieces of fabric. Use a damp cloth when ironing to help the interfacing to adhere to the fabric.

A word of advice: I tried to iron a metre of interfacing to a metre of fabric and ended up in an awful mess.
25cm pieces are just manageable.

Make a cardboard template of
the petal pattern.

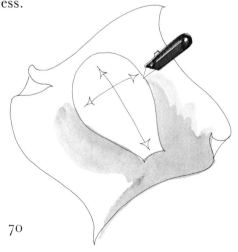

Take one of your pieces of backed fabric and fold it in half. Using the cardboard template, cut three petals out of the folded fabric. You can cut six petals out of one strip of fabric.

Repeat this procedure with each of the remaining strips and you end up with 144 petals.

Putting it Together

Lay the white circular cloth out and pin the petals around the outside edge, with the petal tips overhanging the hem by 5cm (2in). Pin so that each petal overlaps the one next to it by 2·5cm (1in). You will use about 45 petals on the outside edge.

Lay the next row of petals on top, with the tips again overlapping the first row by about 5cm (2in) and each petal overlapping its neighbour by 2·5cm (1in). You should use about 35 petals in this row.

Repeat the procedure for two more rows, using about 26 petals in the

71

third row and 15 petals in the fourth. This leaves a circle in the middle which is about 30cm (12in) across.

Tack all the petals in place starting with the inner ring and working outwards.

Using a zigzag machine stitch and an overall matching cotton, stitch around each petal. When you reach the outside ring of overhanging petals, just continue stitching round the petal tips.

(I tried machining the petals when they were just pinned. I even tried gluing them, but in the end decided that they had to be tacked in place first.)

Middle Circle and Napkins

Measure the circle left in the middle of your petals and, using the extra 2 metre (2¼ yard) piece of fabric, cut a circle (as you did for the cloth) which is 2·5cm (1in) larger in radius than the space that you will be filling. Cut interfacing to fit your circle and iron on.

Cut 2cm (¾in) V notches around the edge and iron under. Don't stitch. Hem this circle, by hand, over the empty centre ring of your petals. Cut your remaining 1·5 metres (1⅝ yards) of fabric into six 50cm (20in) squares. Hem the edges with a machine stitch and use these squares as napkins.

Liberty & Old Lace

Someone once asked me what I collected. I didn't know where to begin. The truth is I never throw anything away! I have buttons and beads, hankies and ribbons, sequins and feathers, bits and pieces of leather and suede, silk and felt, milliner's wire, silver thread and gold leaf paint. It's all there. Waiting.

It is very pleasing to find a use for all the things I've gathered around me over the years and it gave me great pleasure making this waistcoat.

Several years ago, in a scene with John Stride from the television series *Wilde Alliance*, I wore a dress made of pieces of 1920s silks and chiffons. It had all sorts of trimmings in between the materials. I remember thinking it was terrific. I also remember that it caused a certain amount of fuss because it was so expensive. This time, with this waistcoat, there would be no fuss about the expense. All the bits and pieces were *mine*!

Old lace varies in colour from just off white, through cream to rich golden colours. When I laid out some of my old pieces on my bed and looked at them I thought, 'Just like Liberty.' Liberty is my young golden retriever and she is a glorious mixture of all the colours of old lace. The image is only broken by the occasional wayward look on her face: a vagabond in old lace.

With Libby in mind, I got out my Liberty print remnant bags. Liberty's always sell remnants during their semi-annual sales and these are perfect for patchwork.

I live within walking distance of Liberty's on Regent Street. That's one of the joys of living in the heart of London and I still feel a mixture of awe and pride and contentment to walk through Grosvenor Square, past Claridges and Halcyon Days and finally to end up at Liberty's magnificent building. Liberty's didn't begin so grandly. Arthur Lasenby Liberty started his business in half a shop in 1875 and called it East India House. He sold carpets, china, embroidery, lacquer, cloisonné enamel and Satsuma ware, all from the Orient, but even then he concentrated on fabrics.

Liberty imported filmy gauzes from India, fine cottons from the tropics, and silks from China and Japan, but his greatest triumph came when through a partnership with the dyers and printers Thomas Wardle, he introduced 'Art Colours', delicate pastel tints made with new dyes. 'Art Colours' were instantly successful and it was only a matter of time before they became known as 'Liberty Colours'.

'Liberty Colours' were unique and important and strongly influenced the

'Aesthetic Movement' in the late 1800s; by 1881 Gilbert & Sullivan were using Liberty fabrics in their opera productions. Arthur Liberty took such an interest that he sent people to study the clothes in Japan and to bring back exactly what was needed for *The Mikado*.

Liberty didn't rest on his laurels and soon introduced a cashmere called Umritza, a fabric that produced sedate squeals of joy in the press. When Umritza was introduced, *Queen* magazine said, 'There are tints that call to mind French and English mustards, sage greens, willow greens, greens that look like curry, and greens that would be remarkable on lichen-coloured walls and among marshy vegetation – all of which will be warmly welcomed by those who indulge in artistic dress or in decorative revivals.'

Arthur Liberty's success with his fabrics allowed him to move into larger premises and to open a Costume Department where dresses were designed and made in Liberty fabrics and Kate Greenaway's use of Liberty colours in her illustrated *Under the Window* made his fabrics and colours even more famous.

Liberty's alert artistic intuition was not only restricted to fabric. He sensed the importance of the early Art Nouveau movement and as well as commissioning Art Nouveau furnishing fabrics, he also commissioned metalwork, glasswork and ceramics from such illustrious people as William Morris, Walter Crane Ashbee, Rennie Mackintosh and Margaret MacDonald.

When Arthur Liberty died, his nephew Ivor Stewart-Liberty took over the business and in the 1920s created the building that I so much love visiting today. Stewart-Liberty had to fall in line with official planning for Regent Street, but not for Great Marlborough Street. That's why the Regent Street façade is so bland and the Tudor-style Great Marlborough Street side so individual and stylish. It's even more individual and stylish when you discover exactly what went into that building.

All the exposed oak and teak in Liberty's came from two old 'two decker' man-of-wars, HMS *Impregnable* and HMS *Hindustan*. HMS *Impregnable* was built out of over 3000 oak trees, each one over a hundred years old, felled in the New Forest. The next time you want to have a picnic in the New Forest, visit Liberty's!

Liberty's went to equally great lengths to ensure that everything that went in to their new building was of the highest aesthetic quality and it was a rare opportunity, perhaps the last opportunity in this sort of building, for craftsmen to use their skills so fully. External timbers were morticed, tenoned and pegged. All the exterior carving was carried out on site. Each lead paned window had a hand painted picture in one panel.

The sumptuous four storey high inner galleries of Liberty's with their carved balustrades and linenfold panelling were built to resemble the courtyards of old English inns. In total it's a remarkable place, remarkable for the fabrics and articles it has commissioned and sold and remarkable for the environment that has been created in which we can still see and buy such original articles. Liberty's still create outstanding new fabric designs and are recreating some of their original designs from the past. If you are seriously interested in making patchwork (or even if you're not) it is one place that should not be missed.

Instructions

You will need:

1½ metres (1⅝ yards) iron-on fusable cotton interfacing

30cm (12in) of four different Liberty prints

Plus 1½ metres (1⅝ yards) of your favourite Liberty print (for lining)

Bits and pieces of old lace (you can use edges of hankies, lace tray cloths, trimmings, pieces from collars and cuffs, anything, however small. I even used a piece of old satin ribbon)

Lace pins (they are a joy to use, so fine – lovely)

If you don't want to cut your own pattern, Burda No. 7964 is a good basic waistcoat. You can make it as long or short as you like.

Cut the back and two fronts out of the cotton interfacing and lay them out flat, making sure the slightly shiny fusable side is facing upwards. I double-checked this – it would be awful to get to ironing it and find it was the wrong way round! Cut pieces of brown silk to fit the centre panels of the waistcoat and pin them into place on the cotton interfacing (see opposite, top left).

Using three different Liberty prints, cut out three panels for the left side of the top of the back and three for the right side, each 6cm (2½in) wide. Use the fourth print in the middle. Turn in the edges as you pin the panels into place (top right).

Repeat with the bottom panel. For the two fronts, use the same three prints for the panels, top and bottom, making sure where the shoulder seam will be, the patterns match. There will be no triangle at the top (because of the neckline), and you will need a smaller piece of the fourth print on either side at the bottom.

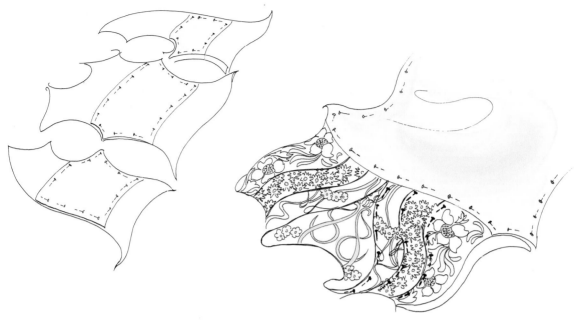

Do not iron. Do not sew. Only pin.

Start putting pieces of lace on the brown silk. When you like the pattern, pin into place. I slipped some in between the Liberty prints. Make sure the side seams of front and back match.

Hand sew the pieces of lace and the edges of the prints into position. Use a tiny running stitch and a creamish coloured cotton thread. Let the stitches show a little; it adds to the charm of it.

Now you can iron it. Use a steam iron if you can, but use a cotton cloth. Don't let the iron come into contact with the brown silk.

The advantage of the fusable iron-on cotton is now clear: the whole waistcoat is firmly interlined. Join the shoulder seams and the side seams. I sewed mine by hand, but you could machine it if you wanted to, it wouldn't spoil it. Open the seams and iron flat (please use your cotton cloth).

Using the same pattern, cut out the lining and sew shoulder seams and side seams. Open them and iron flat.

Take the waistcoat and lining, with wrong sides together, and pin round the armholes and right around both front and back. Sew the two together with a running stitch, removing pins as you sew. Cut off any excess lining. To bind the edges, cut 5cm (2in) wide strips on the bias (across the grain of the fabric) from the remaining pieces of the lining. Hand sew the binding into place round the waistcoat – this fits in with all the other hand sewing.

Sunburst Cloth & Quilt

The rising and setting sun are particularly important in the American Amish home. In the absence of electric lights the woman's treadle sewing machine frequently sits directly inside a window where she will gain the full benefit of the natural light.

Amish is the name given to a Christian group of people who live lives of austerity and simplicity and who believe in separating themselves from the more 'worldly' world. Their magnificent quilts show that even when life is austere, an appreciation for beauty is not lost.

There are many Amish quilt patterns that deal with the sky: the beauty of nature must inspire them. Perhaps their interest in the sky is simply explained by the fact that their working days begin at sunrise and end at sunset.

Sunburst is a pattern obviously based on the sun and stars. It is sometimes called The Rising Sun, Blazing Star or Lone Star.

Amish quilts are easier than most to identify in that they always use dark, strong, vibrant colours and a limited amount of pattern. In the sunburst quilt it's the arrangement of the colours that is most important. There must be a feeling of movement outward from the centre. When the quilter is successful the quilt seems to burst from the centre sending its light out to the ends of the eight points. It is without doubt one of the more ambitious projects in quilt making but the result is so effective that the extra care is worthwhile.

As the name implies the sunburst patterns were nearly always made in sun colours, various shades of red, orange and yellow. It is always a pleasure for me to use red. I love it. I always have. One of my clearest memories from childhood was being given a pair of red shoes. The first patchwork skirt I made I lined with red. My favourite article of clothing is an embroidered Afghanistani skirt about eighty years old that I found in an antique market. It's a wonderful shade of faded red although I would have loved to have seen its colour when it was new. Holly berries, cherries, Coca Cola cans – all red – all irresistible.

Laura Ashley has a wonderful range of plain and patterned fabrics in red and that's where I went for these fabrics. I thought it would be unusual to leave the star shape as it is without backing it and to use it as a table cloth, making a plain red cloth to go underneath.

I have made two cloths for one table before. I have made them plain and patterned, scalloped and ruffle edged. Two cloths always look attractive.

A lace cloth, for example, would be lovely over a plain red one, with the red showing through. If you hunt the jumble sales and antique markets you can often find old lace cloths. They are more difficult to find than they used to be, and more expensive, but if you do what I do and look for damaged ones that can easily be mended or stained ones that can be dyed they are still amazingly cheap. Dyeing is an enjoyable last resort and should be reserved for the cloths that have stains that are impossible to remove. Better a bright red lace cloth than a stained one that sits in the drawer.

I accompanied Bruce to Finland one winter, where he was giving lectures, and experienced an amazing sensation. It was twenty-five degrees below zero at noon each day and the inside of my nose froze! It was the strangest feeling, but it didn't stop me from shopping!

Marimekko had the most stunning display of fabrics in radiant reds and rusts. Blazing Star. Lone Star. Sunburst. They all danced in front of my eyes. I purchased plenty and on my return to London, armed with a sharp new needle in my Bernina, began working on my 'Midnight Sun'. (Well, the fabric did come from Finland!)

I turned it into a giant quilt using unbleached calico and a rust coloured border. That's it on the back of the jacket, as yet unquilted. It will be quilted, however, and I shall quilt diamond shapes out to the edge. Our only problem is that because it's so big we'll need a bigger bed.

Instructions

You will need:

For the star:

1 metre (39in) each of two fabrics (I refer to these as numbers 1 and 2), 122cm (48in) wide

2 metres (2¼ yards) each of three fabrics (I call them 3, 4 and 5) 122cm (48in) wide

Plus if you want to make a cloth:

4 metres (4⅜ yards) red cotton 122cm (48in) wide

4 metres (4⅜ yards) 4oz wadding

8 metres (8¾ yards) red binding

Or if you want to make a quilt:

10 metres (11 yards) unbleached calico (half to appliqué the star on and half to back it)

7·5 metres (8¼ yards) 4oz wadding

Even though the sunburst is one of the oldest patchwork patterns, it can be made using the sewing machine. It is often made in the same way I made Tricia's Garden quilt (see p. 25), hand sewn using papers cut from templates. Machine patchwork can be fun and, of course, very fast, but there are drawbacks. You must be consistent. All seams must be exactly the same and when sewing strips of diamonds together you must check and recheck that the seams cross at exactly the right place. It isn't easy. That said, the sunburst is the most satisfying quilt to make: people's eyes widen when they see it and I like that!

The sunburst pattern is made up of eight diamond-shaped blocks, with 64 diamonds in each block. I used five different fabrics and numbered them in order to plan a design.

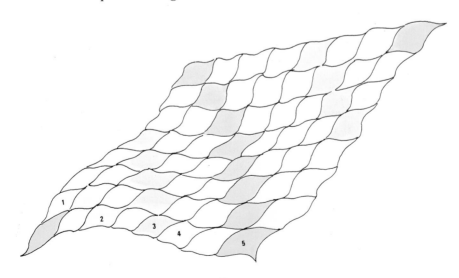

So, you need 10 diamonds of fabric 1
    8 diamonds of fabric 2
    18 diamonds of fabric 3
    14 diamonds of fabric 4
    14 diamonds of fabric 5

There are differences of opinion about cutting out the diamonds. Some people will tell you to cut them out with the straight grain going from tip to tip. Others prefer to cut them with two sides of the diamond on the straight grain.

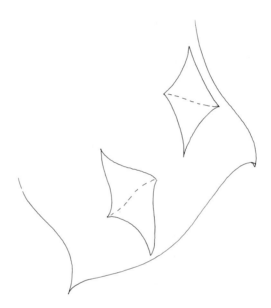

As you can see, with the diamond on the straight grain (right), all four outside edges are on the bias – difficult. You'll always pull one way more than another when you're sewing. On the other hand, with the diamond on the left you have two straight sides, but the middle of the diamond from tip to tip is on the bias – even more difficult. Your blocks will end up being unsymmetrical. Whatever you do, this pattern is one of the most difficult. You must be accurate when cutting the diamonds out and when sewing them together. The problem is not making a block of diamonds – that is fairly easy. But putting the eight blocks together so that they lie flat is not easy. I decided to cut my diamonds on the straight grain, mainly because of the striped material that's in the quilt on the back of the book – I wanted the stripes to run straight up and down. As it worked so well, I cut the ones for the tablecloth the same way.

Lay the diamonds out in your design. Sew the diamonds in the first strip together, then the diamonds in the second strip and so on until you have all eight strips sewn together. Mark them as you go – it would be awful if they got muddled.

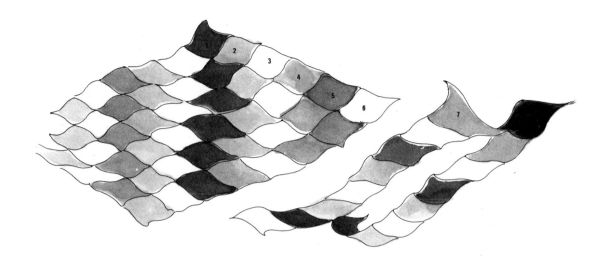

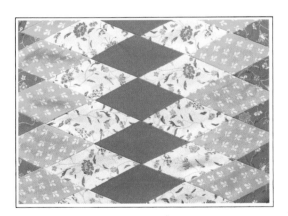

Join strip 1 to strip 2 and so on until they are all joined. You will now have a diamond-shaped block of 64 diamonds. Don't open any seams, but iron them flat, all in the same direction. Make seven more blocks of diamonds. When you have all eight, lay them on the floor next to each other. Sometimes one block fits next to another block better than another.

I don't know why. Sew them together, being very careful to seam away to nothing where they join in the middle.

The star for the cloth measured nearly 2 metres (2¼ yards) by 2 metres (2¼ yards). Join red cotton for the backing and lay it face down on the floor. Lay wadding on top and lay the patchwork star on the wadding.

Pin all round the sides and cut off the excess backing and wadding (there's a lot). Save the pieces of red cotton backing to make napkins.

Stitch all three layers together with a tiny running stitch. I used a satin bias binding for the edges. I wasn't sure that it was a good idea – some people like it, some don't. If I made the cloth again I'd make my own red cotton binding from the backing fabric. Anyway, whatever you choose to use, the edges must be bound.

The star on the back cover of the book I made into a quilt. I joined unbleached calico until I had a piece 213cm (84in) square. I laid the star in the middle and pinned it round. Using a tiny running stitch, I turned the edges of the star in as I stitched it to the calico. I then sewed a band of rust-coloured fabric 10cm (4in) wide to the edge of the calico.

I joined even more calico for the backing and joined wadding to fit. Lay the backing on the floor right side down and lay the wadding on top. Lay the quilt top on the wadding right side up and pin all three layers together on all four sides. As you can see from the photograph, I haven't quilted this quilt yet, but I really must. Now is the time to do it.

Turn the quilt over and cut off excess lining and wadding.

Turn the front of the quilt up over the backing, turn in a small hem and stitch by hand.

Appliquéd Iris Quilt

When my sister Alex got married, I found her an old American quilt with the Rose of Sharon on it. Flower quilts can be tantalising and the delicacy and intricacy of the quilting made this wedding quilt extra special.

Flower quilts are usually appliquéd, mostly with tulips, peonies, dahlias, lilies, sunflowers, poppies, poinsettias and irises.

I didn't really appreciate irises when I was younger; I think I was too preoccupied with being mad about daisies, violets and primroses. It was really interest in the Art Nouveau period which brought the iris to my attention. Just as the more I see David Hockney's tulips the more I like tulips, the more I saw of Art Nouveau design the more I liked irises.

When I decided to grow some I was amazed that there are so many species – over 200 – including the crocus, gladiolus and freesia which are all close relatives. Irises come with and without beards (those coloured hairs on the central line of the petals that fall from the heart of the flower), miniature or

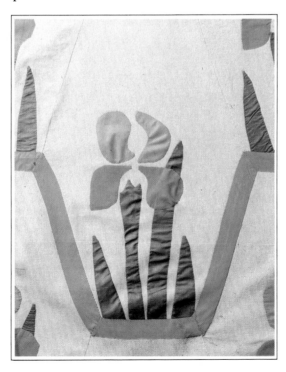

giant, woodland or bog, even Japanese or American. I always thought that the iris was purple but there is a brilliant range of colours, so great that in Greek mythology it was called the 'Rainbow Flower'.

The flower, in fact, is named after the Greek goddess, Iris. Iris was the daughter of Taumas and Electra; she was supposed to be the messenger of the gods and used the rainbow as a way of reaching earth when she had messages to bring. Wherever she trod, the flower that bears her name would grow. I think that's a very appealing legend!

The iris has been used since antiquity for a variety of purposes. The rootstock of certain varieties (*Iris florentina*, *Iris pallida* and *Iris germanica*) was called orris root and was dried and used as a teething ring for babies to keep the teeth white and healthy. It was also chewed to sweeten the breath and fresh orris root was used to treat bronchitis and diarrhoea, even to remove freckles! (I must find out more about that.)

The essence of orris root has a strong smell of violets and was widely used in perfumes. There is even a mention of it in King Edward IV's wardrobe accounts in 1480! It was also used in soap, toothpaste, shampoos, lotions and powders for wigs. Oil of Orris is still used today in pot pourri.

One of the most fascinating uses of the iris is the use of the juice of orris root to give a special flavour to maturing Chianti. The Italians also use powdered root in the making of Iris cake which you can still buy in Florence. Every part of the plant seems to have had some use. Even the leaves are used to produce Iris green, a colouring agent used by artists.

The beauty of the flower itself has always appealed to artists. Durer painted irises in his 'Virgin and Child' and Leonardo da Vinci used them in his 'The Madonna of the Rocks', but their use in art really blossomed, if you will excuse the expression, during the early twentieth century, during the Art Nouveau period. This might be why they were subsequently so popular after World War One, in American quilts.

There are Iris Societies throughout the world. The British one was founded in 1922 and is devoted to the 'encouragement, improvement and extension of the knowledge and cultivation of irises'. The Society publishes a year book that is an unrivalled treasurehouse of iris knowledge.

I found that some irises are easy to grow but that some others have such complicated fertility rites that it's a miracle they can survive at all. My favourite iris is *Iris hoogiana*. It has a classic iris shape and is a wondrous soft clear blue with a golden yellow beard. When I decided to appliqué an iris quilt I chose the delicate blue of this iris rather than the usual shade of purple.

This patchwork is the most time consuming. If you make the iris pieces in your spare time you will find that it can last forever (depending on how much spare time you have) and it would be a mistake to think you could make it quickly. The sewing itself, however, is simple and straightforward. And it's worth the time and effort.

Instructions

You will need:
3 metres (120in) pale blue cotton
1 metre (39in) dark blue cotton } all 90cm (36in) wide
1 metre (39in) green cotton
8 metres (8¾ yards) unbleached calico – (5 metres for the front and 3 for the back), 183cm (72in) wide

I saw a quilt like this in a book of flowered quilts in America. I sent for the pattern, but it took so long coming I started without it! I just copied the picture.

Out of the unbleached calico – oh yes, you must wash the calico first, it shrinks a lot – cut 38 elongated hexagons, leaving a 5cm (¼in) seam allowance as shown below left:

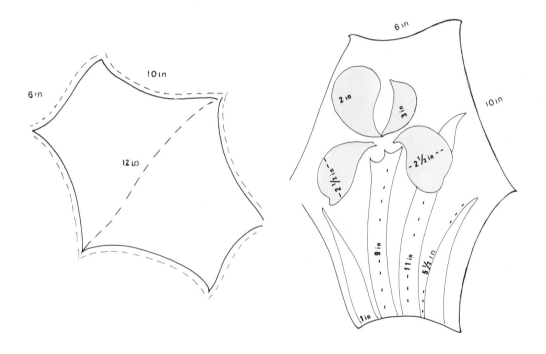

Appliqué 32 of the hexagons with irises. I was very old-fashioned about it all, I just cut a paper pattern of the eight pieces, drew round them on to the fabric, cut them out and turned in the edges as I hand stitched them into place. Above right are the eight pieces with appropriate sizes.

Sew the leaves first and the blue petals next, laying one over the tallest leaf. Use a tiny hemming stitch.

A few months later
Join the appliquéd hexagons together, putting three plain ones top and bottom. You could machine stitch them together as most of the seams will be covered (I didn't).

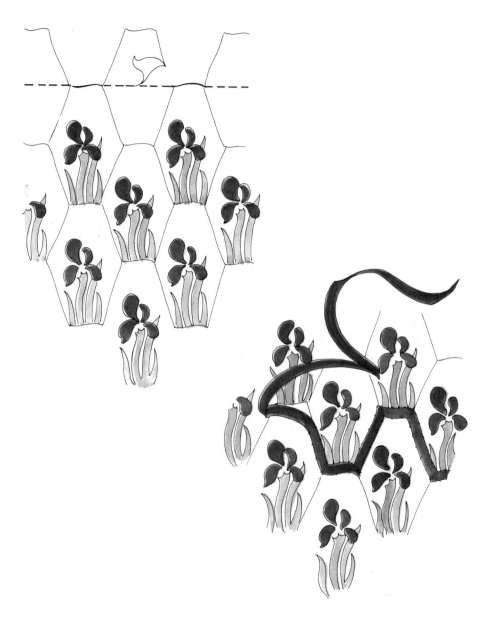

Cut strips of blue cotton 5cm (2in) wide and join them. You want five pieces each 3 metres (120in) long. Iron in a ·5cm (¼in) hem on each side and sew on to the quilt horizontally.

Repeat four times.

When you appliqué a binding like this, you must mitre the corners. When you reach a corner, turn the binding back on itself, make a triangular tuck, turn the binding back to the right side and continue on. You can adjust the tuck to fit the angle you need to turn.

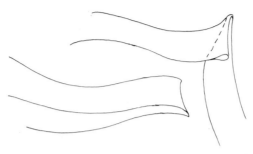

Cut four strips of blue and two strips of calico 183cm (72in) long – for the top and bottom edges.

Cut four strips of blue and two strips of calico 255cm (102in) long for the two sides.

Join two blue strips with a calico strip in between first, and then stitch the band to the edge of the quilt with right sides together.

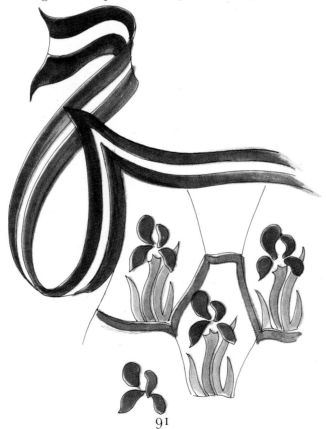

Take the calico for the backing. You'll need it to measure 183cm (72in) by 255cm (102in). Lay the iris cover on the floor right side up, lay the calico backing on top right side down, and pin round all four sides. I didn't use wadding for this quilt. I wanted to see what it looked like hanging on a wall and I thought it wasn't necessary. I was wrong!

Sew the backing and patchwork top together round 3¾ sides, leaving enough open to turn the whole thing right side out. Turn in the edge of the remaining opening and sew closed by hand.

To keep the backing and patchwork in place, I put a small line of running stitches under the seam of the blue overbinding.

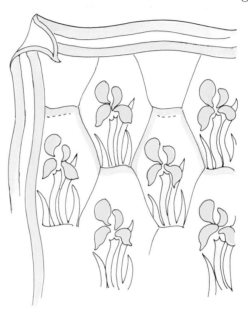

Pink Baskets Quilt

Patchwork began out of necessity. Winters were cold and fabric was in short supply. A careful woman would save pieces of worn out garments and sew them back into a pattern that pleased her, put a layer of cotton or wool underneath and then sew the two layers to a strong backing fabric. The three layers were sewn together with fine running stitches.

Although patchwork quilts were made out of need with fabrics that were recycled, today we view such quilts as works of art. Many of the earliest designs such as the log cabin design used tiny pieces of fabric which meant that almost any scrap could be saved and used. Many a child must have slept beneath a quilt made from remnants of a brother's coat, a father's shirt or a sister's dress. I've seen one quilt in a private home in Florida that was made using empty canvas salt bags for the backing. The owner's grandmother had made the quilt. Her grandfather had been a Mississippi riverboat captain who delivered salt from New Orleans up the Mississippi to Missouri where his family lived. Canvas made a sturdy, lasting backing.

As times became easier, the quilts became more decorative and women were able to choose their patchwork colours and designs more freely. The motifs that appeared reflected daily life; the Carolina Rose, Lincoln's Steps, Cherry Basket, Wedding Ring, Windmill, Grandma's Fan, Barn Door, Drunkard's Path. All these patchwork patterns tell a story. Each one is self explanatory. Patterns were handed down from mother to daughter and from one household to another. Variations appeared from region to region and that's why there is such a wealth of patterns today.

Pieced patchworks generally have an overall design based on repeating a single square. The success of a pieced quilt done in squares depends on colour co-ordination and the positioning of the squares. The development of making one small square or block at a time was economical of both time and space and the work was easier to handle. Mind you, it needed a special eye to visualise the final result when all the small units were joined together. There are literally hundreds of patterns made like this.

Another technique commonly used in the making of bedcovers is appliqué. This is the art of laying one piece of material on the surface of another piece. The pattern is cut out, the edges turned under and it is sewn on using a fine hemming stitch or blanket stitch. This gave scope for making picture quilts of village life or of family trees. Quilts were appliquéd to commemorate import-

ant events: weddings, engagements, a young man's twenty-first birthday (this was known as a freedom quilt) or an anniversary. Friendship quilts were often made by a group, with each square being made by a different woman who often signed the square. (I have one that was made in the first half of the last century. If you hold the quilt up to the light, you can see seeds in the cotton which was used as the batting.) Then they were assembled and quilted for the special occasion. These are also called album quilts.

I thought it would be satisfying to make a quilt in blocks using recycled old cotton sheets. I thought it was a great idea but the way I did it wasn't terribly practical and it gave me awful headaches. I divided the sheets up and decided to dye half of them pink. This is where the first problem began. The worn sheeting I was using was thinner in some areas than in others and this meant that the pink was not even. If you look carefully at the picture you can see how much lighter some bits of pink are.

There are numerous basket patterns to choose from and I mulled over this for some time. In the north of England patchwork baskets and quilted baskets frequently appeared on wedding quilts. Did you know that at one time many people in England were ashamed to admit to having a patchwork quilt because it was considered a sign of poverty? When baskets were used, they were often filled with clematis and grapes – symbols of prosperity and plenty – but I decided to leave my baskets simple.

Having pieced the baskets together, easier said than done, my second problem appeared. I needed to use another sheet to cut out the alternating plain square and do you think I could find one to match? Why was I foolish enough to think that white is white! I tried all my old sheets but nothing was right (or white). The sheet I had used in the basket squares had a definite yellow to it – well cream – off-white.

The piecing of my baskets had taken months and I just had to persevere. I took the creamiest looking old sheet, brewed up a pot of fresh coffee, poured the coffee into the bath, added some water and immersed the sheet. I panicked! It looked too dark, but in fact it turned out that it wasn't dark enough. If you look closely at the picture again you will see the difference in colour between the white in the basket squares and the white in the plain squares.

My third problem was in backing the patchwork and this was the same problem of colour. Yet another shade of white. In the end I bought some fine bleached calico and used that. I ended up purchasing something that looked as if it was recycled.

I thought that the patchwork would look more attractive edged in pink and this is where my fourth problem emerged. I hadn't any dye left and try as I might it was impossible to match it. I tried bias binding, satin binding, ribbon and tape but none was right. I thought of dyeing some of these but my patience was at an end and I simply hand stitched the edges under and left it at that.

So much for my recycling efforts. And I know that my fifth problem is yet to come – I daren't wash it!

Instructions
You will need:
1 metre (39in) plain pink cotton, 90cm (36in) wide
7 metres (7⅝ yards) bleached calico, 99cm (39in) wide
5 metres (5½ yards) 4oz wadding

There are many books of American traditional patterns. If you are going to make a traditional quilt, it's a good idea to have one. There are so many wonderful patterns to choose from and, of course, there would be several basket patterns of one kind or another. I will give you the measurements I used for mine: the sides of each square measure 19cm

(7½in). To start you must make templates of your pattern, using a thick cardboard.

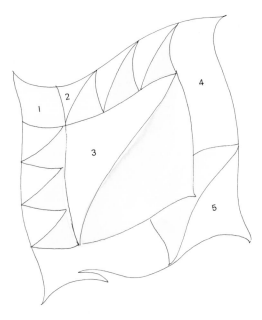

You only need make templates of numbers 1 to 5.

For each square you will need 20 pieces:

    8 small pink triangles – template 2
    1 large pink triangle – template 3
    1 small pink square – template 1
    6 small white triangles – template 2
    1 large white triangle – template 3
    2 white rectangles – template 4
    1 medium triangle – template 5

When you lay your cardboard template on your material, remember you need a seam allowance. Cut ·5cm (¼in) bigger all round.

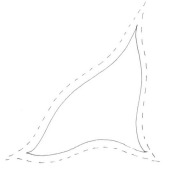

I pieced six small squares of pink and white and one large square of pink and white. Use a tiny running stitch and ·5cm (¼in) seam (opposite left).

Do not iron seams open, just iron to one side. Now sew these squares together, putting the small pink square in the top left hand corner.

96

Sew the remaining five pieces together, as shown opposite.

Sew the two pieces (above right) together. You have a square (at last)!

You need 39 more.

It may be dawning on you that this is no easy project, but all you really need is time. It took me many months to complete the pieced squares. I'll continue . . .

Cut 40 squares of bleached calico the same size as your pieced squares – 19cm (7½in) square. Join them alternately with eight squares across and ten squares down. If by now you are driven mad by all the hand sewing, you could machine them. I thought about this and decided I'd done so much hand sewing I would continue! Iron all seams flat as you go.

Join two 2 metre (2¼ yard) lengths of calico together for the backing. Join two similar lengths of wadding, butt the edges together (see p. 103) and tack across from one side to the other.

Lay your patchwork top on the floor, right side down, and lay the wadding on the top. Lay the calico backing on top of the wadding right side up. Pin all three layers together round all four sides, then sew all round with a running stitch, removing pins as you go.

As with almost all patchwork quilts, this one should be quilted. I stitched round each square and round the pink part of each basket. The plain squares cry out for a lovely quilted pattern. I shall try and do it when I've nothing else to do.

I didn't bind the edges, what with old sheets and dyed pink bits! I just turned under a tiny hem and stitched it by hand. It would look best I think bound in pink, the same pink as the baskets!

Felt Appliqué Quilt

I looked at traditional American quilts, particularly the appliquéd ones that tell stories, for years, before I realised what appealed to me the most. It was that they were made by ordinary people and described their everyday life.

There are many other things that they made that appeal to me: shop signs, weather vanes, decoys, toys, game boards, rugs, child-like portraits of their families and paintings of their houses. These folk artists tell us what people and things really looked like. Some people painted chairs and watering cans, others carved, potted, moulded, stitched and stencilled. They all gave us a more intimate understanding of everyday living in pioneer America.

A question that is often asked is what exactly is American folk art? What does 'folk art' mean? It is often called naïve, a word that seems to imply

primitive, amateur and non-academic. It is certainly characterised by an artistic innocence that separates it from what is presumptuously called 'fine art'. Sometimes folk art is called 'traditional' or 'ethnic' but whatever it's called it comes from the heart and it allows everyday working people to express themselves in the simplest of terms.

Folk art was really the result of American democracy dating from 1776 and it was the next hundred years that saw the best of folk art. The qualities of imagination, inventiveness, design and colour appear in the most unexpected places, tin boxes, pie crimpers, buckets, stencilled floors and painted barns.

The Shelburne Museum near Burlington, Vermont has the most magnificent collection of American folk art. I spent two days visiting it and only saw a fraction of what they have. They have hundreds and hundreds of quilts and I spent a whole day just seeing what they had, never mind actually studying them.

It was at the Museum of American Folk Art in New York City that I first saw the 'Birds of Paradise' coverlet. It's not called a quilt because it was never finished and is in fact just an appliquéd top cover. I was enchanted by it. I loved everything in it, cherries, strawberries, acorns, birds, butterflies, animals, flowers and owls. The female figure near the top is believed to be the maker. The coverlet has been dated (from the appliqué patterns which were cut from old newspaper) as being made between 1858 and 1863 near Poughkeepsie, New York. I never look at it without wondering why she never finished it!

When I decided to make an appliquéd quilt I knew I couldn't just copy the 'Birds of Paradise' cover. It was too personal to the lady who made it, too individual and unique. And so, inspired by her naïve designs, which I loved so much, I have done what folk artists in that first hundred years of American democracy did and, using traditional patterns, made my own style of patchwork.

Instructions
You will need:
1 metre (39in) red felt
1 metre (39in) brown felt
1 metre (39in) beige felt
1 metre (39in) light green felt
1 metre (39in) dark green felt
2·5 metres (2¾ yards) red sheeting for backing
5 metres (5½ yards) 4oz wadding
plus 2·5 metres (2¾ yards) red felt for binding edges
plus as much felt as you need for your design (I used 1½ metres (1⅝ yards) of each colour)
A new machine needle (there's a lot of sewing)

Stick of Pritt glue
B pencil
Drawing pad paper
Any old rough paper for backing squares of felt
Household scissors to cut paper (whatever you do, don't use your
dressmaking scissors – paper makes them blunt)
Matching red, brown, beige, light green and dark green cotton thread

With this quilt the first two decisions were the most important. As the
appliqué would be complicated, I would use felt to avoid having to turn in
all those edges, and I would use only four colours. As you can see, I
couldn't manage with only one shade of green, and I added the odd white
dot.
    I cut 35 squares of felt 30cm (12in) by 30cm (12in):
        8 red
        8 beige
        6 dark green
        6 light green
        7 brown
    Using the Birds of Paradise quilt as a model, I copied my designs on to
drawing paper (it's a little thicker than ordinary paper) and cut them out.
You could trace a design or use a stencil if you wanted to. I used:
        6 squares with flowers
        7 squares with cherries
        6 squares with robins on holly
        5 squares with strawberries
        4 squares with various butterflies
        2 squares with cockerels
        and 1 square each of birds of paradise, dog and cat, owls on acorns,
            girl holding cherries, turkeys.

Take your cut-out paper designs and lay them on the felt. Trace round
the edges with a B pencil (it's softer and blacker) and cut out. Don't be
tempted to cut more than two thicknesses of felt at one time – it never
works, even with thin fabric.
    Back each of your 35 felt squares with any rough paper cut to size and
pin in each corner. (When you stitch your designs on the felt, the paper
keeps it flat. It's very important.)
    With each of your designs you must decide which pieces should be
sewn underneath, and which pieces should be sewn on top. For example,
with flowers the green leaves and stems should be stitched first, the flower
heads next and the middle of the flower heads last. You can make your
designs as complicated or as simple as you like.

To keep your design in place while you sew, stick it to the felt square using Pritt stick glue.

Machine stitch carefully and slowly round all the edges, through the felt square and the paper. Use a matching cotton thread.

To avoid having to change the thread in your sewing machine a million times, sew as much as possible in one colour before changing to the next colour. By the time I had reached this stage I was sewing strawberries and cherries in my sleep.

Remove the paper from the back of the squares. It's a horrible job –
don't rush it, just unpin it and tear it off slowly and carefully.

Arrange your squares ready to sew together. I put five across and seven
down. I didn't have a plan, I just tried not to put the same colour or
design next to each other. I didn't want seams so I sewed them together
by hand. Just overlap the edges and sew with a straight running stitch.
Use matching cotton thread (below left).

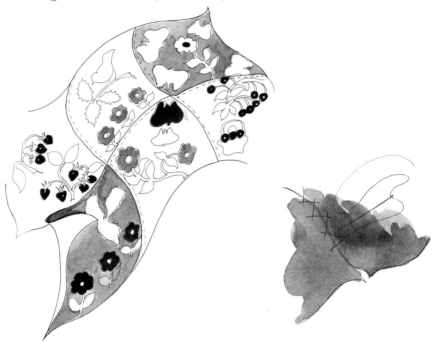

Lay your backing fabric on the floor. I used sheeting (it's wide, so you
don't have to join it). Mine measured 188cm (74in) by 228cm (90in). Lay
the wadding on the top of the backing. It should overlap a little round the
edges. As wadding is never that wide you will have had to join it (above
right).

Lay your felt appliquéd top cover on top of the wadding, right side up.
Making sure all three layers are flat and wrinkle-free, pin round all four
sides. Cut off the surplus wadding and backing fabric.

Sew with a running stitch round all four sides, removing pins as you go.
Make sure you catch all three layers.

I decided to 'tuft quilt' the whole quilt to keep all three layers in place.
I used red embroidery floss and I tied the corner of each square on the
back.

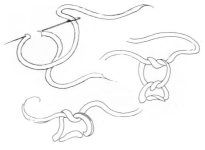

I cut four strips of red felt to bind the edges, two 228cm (90in) by 30cm
(12in), and two 188cm (74in) by 15cm (6in). I bound the sides first,
making the finished width of the binding 12·5cm (5in). The finished width
of the binding at the top and bottom is 5cm (2in).

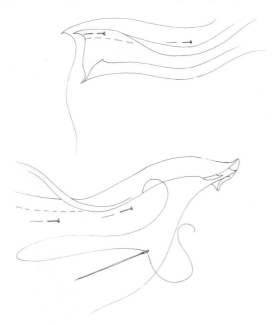

Using brown and beige embroidery floss, I embroidered eyes on the
animals and the face of the little girl.

Harlequin Fancy Dress

Through a pug called Anna, Bruce and I became friends with an elderly couple who lived in Pimlico, an odd and interesting couple who, with the exception of the war years, had spent every August in Venice since the early 1930s.

In 1972, Bruce and I were about to visit Venice for the first time together and were invited to Pimlico to 'receive our instructions'. This couple who loved Venice with a passion and knew it so intimately instructed us on exactly where to go and what to do. We were going there in the late autumn and they told us to stay at Ruskin's old house, on the Zattere facing the Guidecca so that we would get maximum sunlight at that time of year.

We fell in love with Venice. To sit outside in the late afternoon sun and stare at Fortuny's factory, to walk along a narrow way beside the Fenice Theatre and hear a baritone practising his scales, to stand on the Accademia Bridge and see small girls learning ballet in a glass-fronted studio, to rest my eyes on the little dogs painted by Carpaccio in the tiny Scuola di San Giorgio degli Schiavoni, to see the interior of Santa Maria Assunta appearing to be upholstered in green and white damask but in reality all marble, to eat *mollica*, soft-shelled crabs, in out of the way restaurants filled with actual Venetians, to see the light dancing on the mosaics in the cathedral on the lonely and lovely Isle of Torcello, all these things bring an awesome serenity, solitude and tranquillity to life.

We saw pomegranates growing at a mouthwatering restaurant called Locanda Cipriani. Pomegranates grow upside down, it seems! We ate freshly baked florentines. We stared entranced at the gondola repair yard. It would have taken us years to discover all these things gradually by ourselves.

Our friends are no longer alive but I never think of Venice without thinking of them and of the memories that they passed on to us.

Bruce and I try to go for a long weekend each winter. One February we arrived to be faced with children dressed as Columbine, Punch and Pierrot. Men and women were also masked and dressed as Pantaloon, Pulcinella and Harlequin; all characters from early Italian Commedia Dell Arte theatre. We had by chance stumbled upon carnival!

In the eighteenth century, Venice was called the 'carnival city' but like so many beautiful things, carnival slowly faded into a memory. Recently, however, there has been an enormous revival. Dancing in the piazzas. Processions in costume through the calles and along the canals. Fireworks, musical

comedies, Venetian dialect plays, children's fancy dress parades and a traditional final festival in Piazza San Marco itself, with the bells of St Mark's echoing over the city to announce the end of the revels.

We returned to Venice the following year in proper style. Cloaks, black masks, white wigs, tricorn hats and confetti. All Bruce's idea, certainly not mine. He said he felt conspicuous not getting dressed up. I don't. I dress up enough!!

The Italians seem to love their children with an openness and a rich intensity. They certainly dress their children exquisitely, if sometimes rather ludicrously. Bruce took a series of photos of children in fancy dress during carnival and they were wonderful.

In a book about Italian Comedy I saw a drawing of a female Harlequin. It was very striking. I'm not sure, but I think it might have been Columbine in disguise. When Tamara was invited to a fancy dress party I remembered the delight of Bruce's photographs and the uniqueness of the female Harlequin and decided to try my hand at 'Mademoiselle Harlequin'. Tamara's face fell at the sight of the black velvet. She'd rather be a candy floss fairy. 'Please. Wait until I finish it,' I said. As you can see from her face she was quite pleased with it. What a relief!

Instructions

Tamara thought the hooped petticoat was the most important, so I made that first.

You will need:
2 metres (2¼ yards) white cotton 1 metre (39in) wide
2 metres (2¼ yards) broderie anglaise
2 metres (2¼ yards) rigilene
2 metres (2¼ yards) white tape 2·5cm (1in) wide

As it was for a petticoat, I turned the white cotton sideways and cut it to measure 182cm (if you've bought in yards, you'll need all of it). I placed the edges together and sewed a seam.

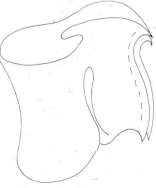

On the wrong side, turn in a 1cm (½in) hem and lay the broderie anglaise edge on it. Lay the 2·5cm (1in) wide tape on top and double stitch.

You are making a pocket to put the rigilene in. When you complete the bottom of the petticoat, leave a gap to slide the rigilene in. When you have done this push the rigilene until the white cotton is pulled tightly and stitch into place.

You can stitch right through rigilene, which is like a synthetic whalebone. It's wonderful for all sorts of things, hats, butterfly wings, rabbits' ears or even mermaids' tails! Thank heaven for John Lewis.

Measure what length you want the petticoat to be. Tamara's was 73cm (29in). Cut off the excess cotton. Turn in a small hem at the top and machine round. Make sure it's wide enough to have the elastic threaded through. On most things for my children I use a wide elastic at least 1cm (½in), if not more. It stays put and I think in the waist it's certainly more comfortable.

Now for the skirt:
You will need:
2 metres (2¼ yards) cheapest black dress velvet, 90cm (36in) wide
2 metres (2¼ yards) black lining, 1 metre 90cm (36in) wide
1 metre (39in) silver lamé
2 metres (2¼ yards) pleated black edging
4 metres (4⅜ yards) silver rickrack braid
Copydex

I decided to ignore all that stuff about velvet, the nap etc. After all, this was just a fancy dress and velvet is expensive. So I used it sideways!

Lay out the 2 metres (2¼ yards) of velvet and cut it into two pieces, one 56cm (22in) wide, the other 36cm (14in) wide.

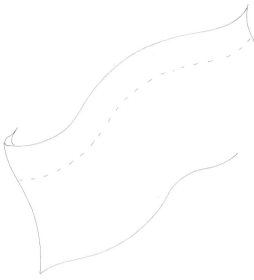

Take your 2 metres (2¼ yards) of black lining and with right sides together join the 56cm (22in) wide piece of velvet and the lining. Do not use the selvage edge of the velvet. Then stitch a side seam.

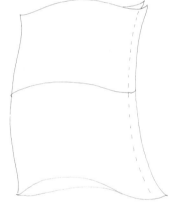

Turn the selvage edge under, lay your black edging on top and stitch round, as you did with the petticoat.

Take your 36cm (14in) wide piece of velvet, turn in each side and machine stitch with a zigzag. This helps prevent it from fraying. Then stitch a side seam.

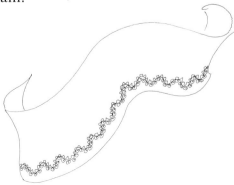

Slide the smaller circle of velvet over the
lining and pin 30cm (12in) up the lining
from the wider piece of velvet, so that
they just overlap.

Machine stitch round and then cut off the excess lining, leaving just
enough above the velvet to make a hem wide enough for your elastic.
There we are – one skirt with two layers, really very easy but it looks very
impressive. I stuck a silver rickrack braid round the edge of the upper
skirt using Copydex.

I cut 9 squares of silver lamé, 19cm (7½in) square, and, using a silver
rickrack braid on the edge of the squares, sewed them on to the skirt.
Make sure you sew through both braid and lamé. This was without doubt
the most frustrating job ever. Velvet and lamé are not a good match
(surprise, surpise). The lamé walks or creeps all over the velvet – trying to
get it to stay in place as I stitched it drove me crazy. So don't think it's
just you. Pin very closely.

For the cloak and hat
You will need:
1·5 metres (1⅝ yards) dress velvet, 90cm (36in) wide
1·5 metres (1⅝ yards) silver lamé
2 metres (2¼ yards) narrow silver ribbon
3 metres (3¼ yards) silver rickrack braid
Cardboard
Copydex

Cut out velvet cloak and silver lining. With right sides together, sew all
round leaving about 15cm (6in) open at the bottom of the back. Pull the
cloak right side out through this space. Sew up by hand. Take the two
strips of silver lamé and join them – the result will be about 254cm
(100in) long. Fold it in half – it's now 10cm (4in) wide. Turn raw edges in
and, using a running stitch gather up until it's a little bigger than the neck

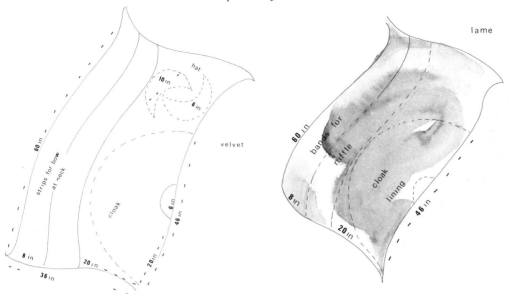

on the cloak. It is like a paper ruffle, so gathered it goes literally haywire.
Put three stitches to hold it in place on the cloak.

Take one of the strips of velvet, fold in half and sew round two sides,
leaving the 10cm (4in) end open to pull it through to the right side.
Repeat with the second piece and sew into place on the neck of the cloak.

Cut a piece of cardboard as thick as you can (I used part of a cardboard box from the supermarket) in the shape of a crescent moon. It should be a little smaller than the cut out velvet pieces. Place the cardboard on the wrong side of one of the velvet pieces and using plenty of Copydex glue, stick the velvet up over the edge of the cardboard. Let it dry.

Now put plenty of Copydex over the edges of the velvet you just stuck and put the other piece of velvet on it, right side up. Turn it over and cut off the excess velvet. Put a little Copydex round the velvet you cut. It dries transparent and stops the velvet fraying.

I stuck silver rickrack braid round the bottom edge of the cloak and along the bottom edge of the hat. I tied two tiny silver bows with very long ends and put them on the points of the hat. Using 2·5cm (1in) wide black elastic I made a hair band and sewed the bottom edge of the hat to it.

Tamara wore a black tee shirt underneath.

Quilted Basket

I find sewing therapeutic. You can think and sew, sort out problems and sew, plan the Sunday lunch and sew, even learn lines and sew. I sew to help me relax in a life that is noisy, hectic, fast, busy and lively.

The pioneer women in America during the nineteenth century didn't have my problems. They lived on isolated farms and homesteads across New England, the great river valleys and the prairies. Many of these women worked on the farms but there was little to stimulate them. One woman is quoted as saying, 'Without my sewing I'd have lost my mind.'

If this individual sewing was therapeutic, then the quilting bee must have been like a form of group therapy. A group of women would gather together to quilt and gossip over the quilting frame. Quilting bees were often held in the winter, would last all day and would end with eating and dancing.

There are two types of decorative quilting. In Trapunto quilting, the outline of a shape is stitched through two layers of material and wadding is inserted from the back. This is sometimes called stuffed quilting. In Italian quilting two layers of material are stitched together in narrow parallel lines and a cord is threaded through between these lines to raise the surface.

The traditional quilting stitch is a fine running stitch. A good measure is to make six to nine stitches per inch depending on the thickness of the quilt. A frame really is necessary for accurate quilting and it is quite easy to make, using lengths of wood one inch by two inches and as long and as wide as your quilt. The four pieces of wood should be clamped or otherwise held together and the resulting frame placed on four chairs.

Before you can start quilting, the backing material must be thumbtacked to your frame, tacking one side, then the opposite, making sure it is taut and then repeating the procedure for the other two sides. Once this is done the batting or wadding should be laid on the backing, making sure that it overlaps all sides.

Finally the patchwork top is laid on the batting and all three layers are then basted together along all four sides of the frame. As the quilting progresses, remove two clamps from one side, roll the quilt up on the length of wood, removing the thumbtacks from the side lengths of wood as you go. Then reclamp the frame and continue quilting.

Alternatively you can use a quilting or embroidery hoop for quilting: with this method you lay the three layers on the floor and, making sure that there are no wrinkles, baste across the middle of the quilt as well as the sides. When a hoop is used, the quilting should start in the middle and work outwards towards the edges.

A sewing machine can be used for quilting if you have neither the space for a frame nor the time for hand quilting and when you use a machine, use a straight stitch with a stitch length of nine to twelve stitches per inch. The thread tension should be adjusted according to the thickness of the quilt.

Hand quilting, though time consuming, is very rewarding. You can look back on your work later with the satisfaction that you made every stitch yourself. All patchwork really should ultimately be quilted one way or another.

Instructions
You will need:
A basket
1 metre (39in) Liberty print, 90cm (36in) wide
1 metre (39in) thinnest bleached calico, 99cm (39in) wide
1 metre (39in) 2oz wadding – the lightest
A metre (or yard) ruler if you have one
Pencil
See-through nylon thread

Iron the calico, it must be flat. If you have a table big enough, lay it on it and blutack the four corners, just to keep it still. (Blutack is fantastic, but don't put it on anything you might mark.)

Using your ruler and pencil, mark out a diagonal grid to stitch by later. Start by marking 2·5cm (1in) intervals all the way round.

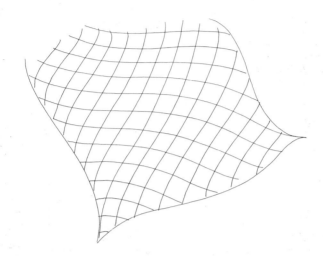

Lay the metre (39in) of Liberty print on the table, right side down, cut off a strip 5cm (2in) wide and put it aside to use later. Lay the metre (39in) of wadding on top. Now lay the piece of marked calico on top of the wadding and pin round all four sides. Do not sew. If you are going to hand quilt, use a hoop and start in the middle. Follow the pencil lines with a tiny running stitch catching all three layers. If you decide to machine quilt, which I did, sew with a slightly loosened stitch following the pencil marks. Make sure it all stays flat. When you reach the edges, remove the pins.

My first attempt at quilting was very disappointing. For both hand and machine quilting it really is a question of practice. If you haven't done it before, hand sewing is likely to be more successful unless you are a real whizz with your machine. I should mention that Liberty's sell some of their prints already quilted, but I've always wanted to 'do it myself'.

Using a piece of paper, make a pattern of the inside shape of your basket. Do the bottom separately. Lay the pattern on your quilted fabric and cut out. Don't forget to make an allowance for any seams. The edge that will be at the top of the basket should be turned under and stitched all round. Take the quilted piece of fabric for the bottom of the basket and sew it, right sides together, to the rest of the lining (below left).

Slip the lining into your basket and using a large needle and double transparent thread sew the top edge of the fabric to the edge of the basket. You really can't see the thread – you can go round the woven bits of basket and back through the fabric (below right).

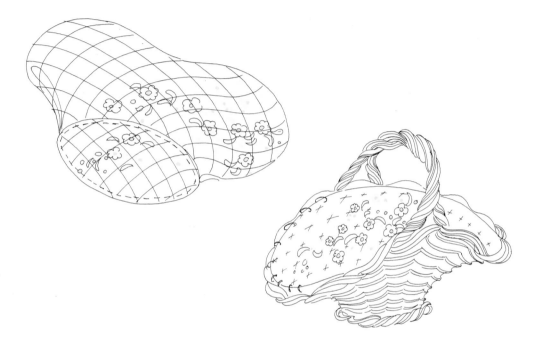

Now I took the 5cm (2in) strip of Liberty fabric that I'd cut off to start with. I ironed in a hem on each side of it and wrapped it round the handle and tied a bow.

I just happened to have a few bits of felt in the right colours. I cut them into flowers, cutting the leaves with pinking shears. I don't use them very often, but when I do it's such fun. I stuck the flowers with Copydex and sewed them on to the fabric round the handle.

Kite

Why is it that people who fly kites are so nice? I know that's a silly statement; like saying that people who walk dogs are all nice but come to think of it, all the people I know who fly kites also walk dogs! My brother-in-law Derek is an inveterate Parliament Hill kite flyer, a perfect dog walker and as nice a person as you would ever wish to meet, my stereotype of a kite flyer. (His dogs are pretty good too.)

I knew nothing about kites or the history of kites until I decided to make one. I have always felt that one of the extra pleasures of acting has been the interesting information and knowledge that you are exposed to along the way.

If I ever have to fly a kite in a future production a lot of the normal preliminary work has been done. I will first of all suggest that my character has a dog. I will also equip her with David Pelham's book, *The Penguin Book of Kites*. I found it both practical and informative. I'm told it's called the kiters' Bible.

It is a safe assumption that the Chinese invented the kite almost 3000 years ago. They certainly had the necessary materials. Bamboo cane was in plentiful supply and silk has been made in China for 4500 years.

By the eighteenth century kite flying was a popular pastime with children and adults throughout Europe but inquisitive minds were still conducting experiments with kites. Benjamin Franklin, who might be best known now for his face on the American five dollar bill, attached metal keys to kites and flew them in electrical storms so that he could learn more about electricity.

By the nineteenth century, scientific minds had become obsessed with flight and kites took on new significance. Now you might think that Alexander Graham Bell was only concerned with inventing the telephone, but he wasn't. In Canada he built kites with engines and founded the 'Aerial Experiment Association' whose sole purpose was to put men into the air. And he succeeded. Some of his kites can still be seen at the Bell Museum in Baddeck, Nova Scotia.

Meanwhile, back in England, B. F. S. Baden-Powell, the chief scout's brother, was achieving fame by becoming the first Englishman to lift a man with a kite. He wanted kites to be used in military aerial observation.

Chinese and Japanese kites have much more romance about them and Asian folklore abounds with stories involving kites. Even today in Japan, on the fifth day of the fifth month of each year the Boys' Festival is celebrated and families who have had sons in the previous year fly brightly coloured kites from poles to honour the birth. The kite is usually shaped like a fish and specifically a carp. The carp battles upstream each year to spawn and represents strength and the ability to overcome overwhelming odds. The bright fish-shaped kite standing in the wind symbolises the son's progress through the river of life. It might be sexist only to fly the fish kite for sons but I still love the idea behind it.

In Korea it is still the custom in some areas to write the name and birth date of each son born (here we go again) on a paper kite and when the kite is flying high to release it to drift away as far as possible. The drifting kite is supposed to draw away bad luck and evil spirits from the newborn son. In Malaysia, kites were flown to celebrate the clear, fresh blue skies that followed the rainy season. The history and shape of the Malay kite appealed to me, so that is what I made.

I had never made a kite before, so I decided I would do exactly what I was told to do. I read all sorts of instructions (enough to put anyone off) and took advice from a young man called Andy King. He really loves kites and was happy to talk at length about the hazards involved in making a kite and how to avoid them. He is to be found in 'The Kite Store' in Covent Garden, together with a terrific dog and some inspiring kites. Everything you need for making and flying kites is available from their mail order.

Anyone can make a kite, I was told, but it must fly. I was given endless advice which I'll pass on to you as I go along. The first advice was to make a simple, straightforward kite, I could mess about with it later. Cheek!

Instructions
You will need:
3 metres (3¼ yards) navy blue ripstop (that's what kites are made of)
·5 metre (20in) each pink, yellow, black, white and red ripstop
6 metres (6½ yards) narrow nylon ribbon
·5 metre (20in) thick cotton tape
3 wooden struts like sweet pea sticks
    1 149cm (58½in) long
    2 74cm (29in) long
1 dihedral piece (a bent piece of aluminium to bow the kite)
3 rings
Size 70 sewing machine needle
Matching *polyester* threads

When you look at the front of a Malay kite it bows away from you. When the back is facing you it bows towards you.

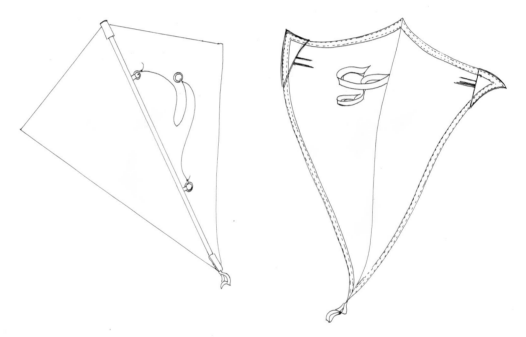

Using a saw, I cut three pieces of wood – 1 piece 149cm (58½in) long and two 74cm (29in) long. I was surprised to find it was quite easy.

Cut the 3 metre (3¼ yard) piece of navy ripstop in half. Lay the two pieces out and cut one half of the kite from one piece and the other half from the second piece. The reason for this is you want the selvage on the inside of each half. If you buy material in yards, you'll need a bit extra so that you can cut a 58½in piece out of each half.

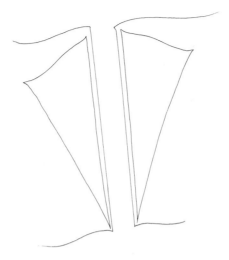

For a kite to fly, it must be absolutely symmetrical. You mustn't turn in more of an edge on one side than the other, or double stitch more on one side than the other. It must measure and weigh exactly the same on each side of the centre strut. Cut two pieces of nylon ribbon each 5cm (2in) long, put a ring on each piece. Lay out half your kite and pin one piece of ribbon with a ring on it 24cm (9½in) from the top and the other 47cm (18½in) from the bottom, both rings facing outwards.

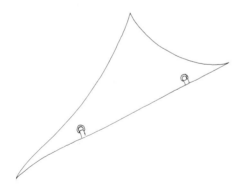

Lay the other half of the kite on top and using a slightly thinner needle than usual (I used a 70) and matching *polyester* thread, sew a narrow seam ·5cm (¼in) wide. Turn the kite right side out and fold in half. Pin a centre seam 1·5cm (½in) wide. You are making a pocket to put the centre strut in. After you have pinned the seam, check that the 149cm (58½in) strut will slide into it. If the strut fits, take it out and put it away until later. If not, you've pinned the seam too tight – adjust it until the strut does fit. Cut a piece of nylon ribbon 51cm (20in) long and fold in half. Place it directly opposite the top ring. Slip the folded end of the ribbon into place and pin. Sew the seam (below left).

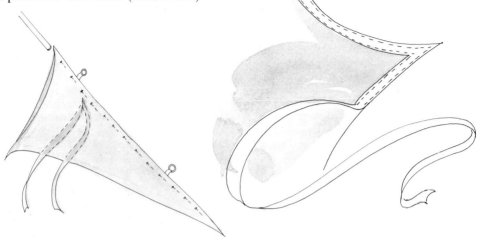

On the back of the kite, turn in ·5cm (¼in) all the way round, lay the nylon ribbon over and double stitch (above right).

This is the beginning of a lot of double stitching. I was told it was a good idea, otherwise the wind would just rip the kite apart!

To make the wing tip pockets, cut two pieces of navy ripstop 30cm (12in) long and 15cm (6in) wide. Fold in half so that the 30cm (12in) is now 15cm (6in), fold again the other way and you have a piece of ripstop 15cm (6in) by 7·5cm (3in) and four layers thick. Still on the back of the kite, lay the four thicknesses on the wing tips and double stitch on the edge. Cut off the excess (below left).

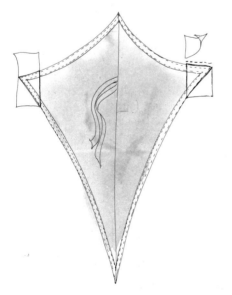

Cut two 10cm (4in) pieces of the thicker cotton tape to protect the top and bottom of the centre strut. Fold in half and sew in place over the top of the centre seam (opposite, bottom right).

You don't do the bottom pocket until the kite is completely finished. I decided to assemble the kite, to make sure that so far it was all right. I slid the centre strut into the centre pocket and pinned the bottom so that it wouldn't fall out. I put the two smaller struts into the aluminium piece and slipped the other ends in the wing tip pockets. Slide the piece of aluminium up until you find your ribbon and tie firmly. The kite is now bowed towards you.

Well, so far, so good. Now for the fun part, I thought, messing about with it. Untie the ribbon and remove the wing struts and aluminium piece. Unpin the bottom of the centre seam and slide the centre strut out. You are left with a flat kite, a plain flat kite.

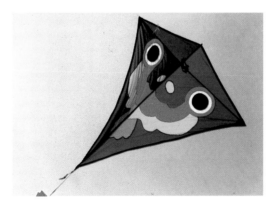

Matsutara Yanase, a famous kite maker, made a kite like an insect called a cicada. The cicada has transparent wings and chirps on hot summer days. I would try and make an insect face. I was told on no account to touch the edges of the kite I had made. I was to cut up and stitch only within the framework.

I decided to appliqué my design separately, then I would have just one piece to lay on to the kite.

I cut six circles: two pink 27cm (10½in) across, two white 20cm (8in) across and two black 14cm (5½in) across. Lay a white circle in the middle of a pink circle and double stitch round with white polyester thread, turn it over and cut away the pink ripstop next to the stitching.

Now lay the black circle in the middle of the white circle, and double stitch around with black thread. Turn it over and cut away the white ripstop within the stitches. You have an eye. Now make another one with the remaining three circles. I cut a piece of pink, a piece of yellow and a piece of red and joined them all by double stitching. I then added the eyes.

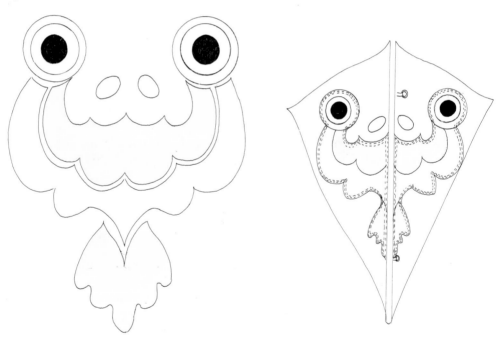

I now had one piece. I carefully cut it in half and pinned half on one side of the centre pocket, and half on the other side. I double stitched it using matching thread.

Turn the kite over and cut away the navy blue ripstop close to the stitching. Hold it up to the light, it's fantastic when you see the light coming through those colours. As you can see, I added a nose, just two little bits of yellow! Slide your centre strut into its pocket and pin the bottom. Take the piece of thicker cotton tape that you have already cut and make a protective cover as you did at the top. I was told to leave one side half stitched. If ever your wooden strut breaks – heaven forbid – you slide the pieces out and slide a new one in. On the front of your kite are two rings. You need a piece of kite-flying line 178cm (70in) long tied from one ring to the other. This is the bridle. Your third ring ties on to this, for your flying line to be fixed to.

Oh, I nearly forgot the tail. First cut a piece of nylon ribbon 7·5cm (3in) long, fold it in half and sew into place by hand: it should be at the bottom of the centre strut, making a little loop. You tie the tail on to it. Cut strips of ripstop 5cm (2in) wide and join them until you have at least 10 or 12 metres (30 or 40 feet). Put a coloured bow shaped piece 22·5cm (9in) long and 10cm (4in) wide, every foot. It looks gorgeous.

Flying your kite

If you have put as much time and trouble into making your kite as I did, please make sure you don't destroy it the first time you fly it. In London it seems that everyone with kites flies them at Parliament Hill in Hampstead, but a more ideal landscape is flat, without the hazard of tall trees, electricity pylons and power cables. It is illegal to fly a kite within three miles of an airport and there are local regulations regarding height.

It is easiest if two people launch the kite. One holds the reel and stands with his back to the wind. The other stands fifty feet away and holds the kite by its towing ring. Lay the tail of the kite on the ground towards the person holding the reel because as the kite lifts up this has an immediate effect on stabilising it. The person holding the kite should release it from arm's length and the wind will lift it into the air.

Don't let the line out too quickly once the kite is airborne. Pull on the line as the kite rises, then slowly release a bit of it, continually pulling and releasing until the kite is high in the sky.

Ben was more worried about the kite flying than I was and even more worried about it crashing. (I think he might write disaster movie scripts when he grows up.) When the kite was flying well we both sighed with relief. I can't remember ever having felt such a sense of achievement.

Kite flying is exhilarating; feeling the kite tugging on the line and watching it dancing in the sky gave me a marvellous sense of well being and great satisfaction. Ben said it felt like having a twenty pound salmon on his fishing line. From an ardent fisherman this is the greatest praise.

Words of Advice

1. When making patchwork there is only one piece of advice that really matters. Be accurate. Measure, cut and sew accurately. Almost all problems with patchwork arise because of inaccuracy.

2. Always wash fabrics before you use them, particularly cotton, calico and linen which you know will shrink.

3. Choose your colours very carefully. It's the most important decision you'll have to make. The use of colour plays an enormous part in the success of a quilt. So spend time and trouble on the planning. Remember the actual sewing is only half the project.

4. Don't use your best fabric scissors to cut paper – you will ruin them. I have separate paper scissors and they are marked.

5. If you are starting a project that involves a lot of machine sewing, make sure your machine is in good order. Have it serviced if you think it needs it. A little cleaning and a little oiling goes a long way. After oiling, sew a few stitches through a piece of blotting paper just to be sure there's no oil left that might get on your fabric. A new needle is a good idea – it's amazing how lovely and sharp a new needle is.

6. If you are making a quilt or anything large, there is much 'laying it on the floor'. I put a large old sheet on the floor, just to be safe.

7. When you cut out the paper patterns for traditional patchwork (see Tricia's Garden, p. 25), don't cut out more than four at a time. If the paper is very thick, then two is the limit. They will never be accurate enough if you attempt more. The same applies to the fabric pieces. I usually cut out two at a time.

8. When quilting by hand or sewing patchwork pieces together, run your cotton thread through beeswax. It will strengthen it and stop it twisting. Ann Ladbury makes a good neat piece of beeswax especially for this purpose.

9. Do you drop pins or spill the whole box? At the end of a day sewing I find pins everywhere. A pin magnet is such a time-saver. Ann Ladbury also makes one of these (she's fantastic).

10. If you want to hem a fine or delicate fabric that you don't want to mark with pins, hold the fabric in place with hair grips. If you must use pins, then use super-fine lace pins.

11. If you are using a paper pattern of any kind, iron it first with a cool iron to take the creases out, then you can be sure of being accurate (there's that word again).

12. If you are going to appliqué with the machine, using a straight stitch (see felt appliqué quilt, p. 99) don't try and stitch more than three stitches at a time. That way you can do perfect circles (with a bit of practice). I found this advice in an American book on sewing appliqué and thought, 'Three stitches, that's ridiculous.' But it's absolutely right and I am grateful for it. Also remember never to stop with the needle up – it must be down, sunk into the work, so that you can move it round ready to continue.

13. With all kinds of appliqué, use Vilene Stitch 'n' Tear on the back instead of paper. It's much easier to remove. I wish I'd used it when I made the felt appliqué quilt. You could use it on the simple quilt (p. 9) as well.

14. To save time and screaming with frustration when machine stitching a quilt, thread up two or even three underspools of thread, so you have a replacement ready waiting when one runs out.

15. Whatever you do, don't keep any good linen or lace in a warm airing cupboard. It will ruin it by discolouring it amazingly quickly. Wrapping it in dark blue tissue paper will stop it yellowing.

16. The accidents I have had with the iron! It's so easy to ruin a piece of fabric with one move. I have learnt to use a cloth all the time, on everything. I have a piece of butter muslin which is perfect – it's very thin and you can see through it.

17. Robin (you know, he makes starch) also makes some wonderful stuff called Fabulon. Not only does it make ironing easier, but everything looks so much better. I iron everything with it. It gives body without being starchy stiff. You really must try it.

18. If you can't find something you want or want to know something – ask. There's always someone around delighted to help. There's a wonderful woman called Olive at John Lewis in Oxford Street who spends all day sorting out everyone's sewing problems.

19. Some projects involve many months work. It's possible there will be a time when you hate the sight of it and never want to see it again (guilty). Whatever you do, don't put it away. It may be five years before you get it out again (guilty again). Just leave it in a heap somewhere so you have to climb over it now and again. You'll finish it if only to get it out of the way.

20. Don't throw anything away!

Glossary

Patchwork sewing pieces of material together to form a flat, unbroken surface.

Appliqué a French term meaning the sewing of one fabric on top of another.

Backing the piece of fabric used on the underside of a quilt.

Basting or **Tacking** large running stitches put in to keep the fabric in place prior to proper sewing.

Binding the process used to cover the edges of the work, sewing and holding them together.

Block patchwork a block, sometimes square, made of a number of patches and subsequently joined together with others to make a quilt.

Broderie anglaise an open embroidery on white linen.

Butting you butt batting or wadding together when you want a larger piece. The edges fit side by side, not overlapping, as this would make a bump.

Floss untwisted silk thread for embroidery.

Grain the arrangement of threads (cross and lengthwise) in woven fabrics. *Straight grain* runs parallel to the selvage. *Cross grain* runs from selvage to selvage. *Bias* is the diagonal that intersects the straight and cross grain.

Hexagon the most popular patchwork pattern. It has six sides.

Iron-on fusable cotton Cotton fabric that sticks to whatever it's steam-ironed to.

Piecing sewing together patchwork shapes with a seam to make a block or an overall design.

Quilting tiny running stitches taken through three layers of a quilt.

Raw edge the unfinished edge of a fabric.

Rigilene synthetic whale bone used for stiffening.

Raised patchwork another name for puff patchwork (see p. 61).

Selvage the finished edge of a piece of fabric, generally more tightly woven than the rest of the fabric.

Template a patchwork shape or pattern cut from a durable material such as cardboard. The ones you buy are either plastic or metal.

Trim cut away excess fabric.

Tuft quilting a piece of thread (sometimes embroidery floss) sewn through three thicknesses of a quilt and then tied.

Under spool the small metal cotton reel that holds the underneath thread of the sewing machine.

Wadding or **batting** a bonded polyester padding for putting between a patchwork top and a lining or backing. There are three different weights, 2oz, 4oz and 8oz. It also comes like cotton wool in bags for stuffing toys and puff patchwork.

Zig-zag a machine stitch, a succession of straight line stitches going from side to side.

Useful Addresses

I bought fabrics from:

Liberty's & Co
Regent St
London W1

Designer's Guild
277 Kings Rd
London SW3

John Lewis
Oxford St
London W1
(and branches up and down the country – they're marvellous. The fabric and accessories for over half the projects in this book came from there.)

Laura Ashley
183 Sloane St
London SW1

The Upstairs Shop
22 Pimlico Rd
London SW1

Ann Ladbury has done so much to encourage everyone to sew. She's fantastic. She's produced a range of sewing tools to make life easier. I use many of them including a fade-away fabric marker, magnetic pin catcher, beeswax, tacking thread and a tweezer bodkin. These are available from many stores and by post from:

Harlequin
Unit 2s
Jubilee End
Lawford
Manningtree
Essex.

Other addresses I found useful:

Joen Zinni-Lask
The Patchwork Dog and Calico Cat
21 Chalk Farm Rd
London NW1
(for anything to do with traditional patchwork, books, patterns, information on courses and lovely old quilts)

The Wheatsheaf
54 Baker St
London W1
(for Stabilo pens or *anything* to do with art)

The Pentonville Rubber Company
48 Pentonville Rd
London N1
(for almost anything rubber, or foam cushions cut to any size or shape)

The Button Box
44 Bedford St
London WC2
(for buckles and buttons)

The Bead Shop
39 Neal St
London WC2
(for fantastic beads)

The Hobby Horse
15/17 Langton St
London SW10
(for beads, buttons, templates and all sorts of sewing accessories)

Jem Patchwork Templates
Forge House
18 St Helen's St
Cockermouth
Cumberland
(for every kind of template)

The Midland Educational
104 Corporation St
Birmingham 4
(a shop I would dearly love to be near. They seem to have everything for crafts and a fantastic bookshop where you can actually find what you're looking for. They also have stationery and art supplies – and a charming and well-informed staff)

The Kite Store
69 Neal St
London WC2
(will tell you everything you need to know about making a kite – and more. They also have a mail order catalogue)

The Quilters Guild
'Clarendon'
56 Wilcot Rd
Pewsey
Wiltshire
SN9 5EL

The Embroiderers Guild
Apartment 41A Hampton Court Palace
East Molesey
Surrey
KT8 9AU

Both these guilds are open to all; they have wonderful facilities and hold classes, workshops and exhibitions. The Embroiderers Guild has over 100 branches in the UK.

For all sorts of craft books, write to:

The Search Press
Wellwood
North Farm Rd
Tunbridge Wells
Kent

If you want to know more about irises, write to:

The British Iris Society
67 Bushwood Rd
Kew
Richmond
Surrey
TW9 3BG

To discover more about American Folk Art visit:

The Museum of American Folk Art
125 West 55 St
New York
N.Y.10019
U.S.A.